SHOUTYKID

How Harry Riddles Made a MEGA-amazing Zombie Movie

by
Simon Mayle

Illustrated by Nikalas Catlow

HarperCollins *Children's Books*

First published in Great Britain by HarperCollins *Children's Books* 2014
HarperCollins *Children's Books* is a division of HarperCollins*Publishers* Ltd,
77-85 Fulham Palace Road, Hammersmith, London W6 8JB

Visit us on the web at
www.harpercollins.co.uk

3

SHOUTYKID – HOW HARRY RIDDLES MADE A MEGA-AMAZING
ZOMBIE MOVIE
Text copyright © Simon Mayle 2014
Illustrations copyright © Nikalas Catlow 2014
Simon Mayle and Nikalas Catlow assert the moral right to be
identified as the author and illustrator of this work.

ISBN: 978-0-00-753188-2

Printed and bound in England by
Clays Ltd, St Ives plc

MIX
Paper from
responsible sources
FSC www.fsc.org **FSC® C007454**

For my boys, Ayrton & Pelé. U kids rock.

GrRRR
splurp

my pet
zombie

From Harry Riddles **to** Charley Riddles
Subject: World of Zombies and other stuff
5 January 20:04 GMT

Hi Cuz –

Sorry I can't write to you on Facebook, because guess what? My mum found out I opened my own account over Christmas and she said I'd better close it or I could get in a LOT of trouble. My sister said kids like me can go to prison for opening new Facebook accounts. Well, I'm only ten – I don't need that.

Good news is, my dad said now he's got a wood burner out in his office I can use his laptop, which means you and me can email each other, which is gonna be really **GRRRREAT**, right?

My dad also said if we do start writing, then maybe I won't spend so much time in my room gaming, cos he thinks gaming is a waste of my life and stops me making new friends and doing all the stuff he thinks kids like me should be doing, like skateboarding, or learning to surf, or playing sports or whatever – but basically that's never gonna happen, cos **I REALLY, REALLLLLLLLY LOVE GAMING!!!!**

BTW – have you played WORLD OF ZOMBIES? I got given this game for Christmas and if you haven't played it, you should definitely GET it. I know you guys are like eight hours behind us time-wise in California, but if you can get out of your bed before... let's say lunch on a Saturday morning (which I know is a big ask), then you and me could easily game for an hour or more before my mum tells me to brush my teeth and go to bed and stop shooting zombies. So if you wanna play, let me know your gamer tag, then I can add you to my list of friends, OK? Cool!

How was Christmas out in California? Sunny? It rained here. My dad said it hasn't stopped raining in Cornwall for like five years now and the last time we had more than a week of straight sunshine was maybe in the last century. He also said if things carry on the way they're going we'll all be swept back down to the sea in a GIANT FLOOD, which he thinks is maybe a good thing, cos life would be a LOT easier if we were fish, cos fish don't owe the bank lots of money and we do.

Other than that not much has changed since you guys were here. My mum still makes big art animals in the barn for rich Germans, but she's thinking she may have to get a job at my school teaching if they stop buying. I don't want that to happen cos that'll make my life even MORE embarrassing with Ed Bigstock. You know the kid

I talked to you about? His dad is a polar explorer but he's a pain in the butt? Him.

Plus, I still really hate Charlotte. She's now almost sixteen and I try and stay out of her way as much as possible, but the good news is she has just got her first real boyfriend, who has HIS OWN CAR, which means they go out a lot (if my mum gives them petrol money). His name is Spencer and he's an eighteen-year-old gap-year kid, who teaches music at my school. With any luck they'll get married soon and emigrate to Australia and then my life will be a whole lot easier because my sister still hates me too.

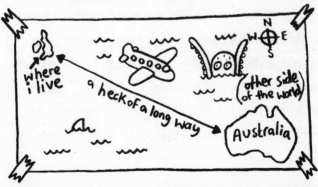

The other good news is, our dog has not got stuck down a rabbit hole for like three weeks now, and my dad has just finished his new movie script, which means when he sells it, we're going to come out to California and stay with you guys, which will be really, REALLY great and I can't wait!

OK. That's it. Your turn.

Harry

From Charley **to** Harry

11 January 09:14 PST

Smurf

What are you doing making your dad call
my dad to find out why I haven't written? I
don't have the time. I'm an athlete. I have to
practise. But my dad says if I don't write to
you, he'll take away my Xbox, my iPad and
my phone. So here you go. Here's my letter.
OK? There! Bye!

Charley

From Harry **to** Charley
11 January 17:27 GMT

That's all you have to say? You could at least tell me how the weather is.

Harry

From Charley **to** Harry
11 January 11:42 PST

You know how the weather is. It's sunny because it's ALWAYS sunny in California. That's why it's called the Sunshine State. And BTW – I REALLY don't have the time to keep writing to you, OK. So please leave me alone.

Charley

From Harry **to** Charley
12 January 09:19 GMT

That's funny cos my dad says your dad says you're either in bed SLEEPING all day when you're not at school, or you're online all night shooting terrorists with your friends. But if you're too busy to write, I get it. Thanks anyway for putting all that effort in. It's really great to hear from you – even if it was only like two lines. Anyway, I know all your news. My dad said you'd won this big lacrosse tournament in California, which meant that your school was the best lacrosse school in the whole of America, which is pretty incredible cos in England only GIRLS play lacrosse. Boys play RUGBY. So congratulations on being the best at that. I mean it.

Harry

From Charley **to** Harry
12 January 10:11 PST

Hey –

I don't know where you get your news from
but lacrosse is a MAN'S sport in America,
not a GIRL'S sport, OK? And cos we won
the tournament and cos I got voted MVP
(that means Most Valuable Player, which
is something you'll probably never achieve
in your loser life) I'm going to get a college
scholarship to play my MAN'S sport at a top
Ivy League school, which is A PRETTY DARN
GOOD THING. So stick that in your pipe
and SMOOOOOKKKKE IT, you
little dweeb! Your slick, game-
winning, MVP cousin,

Charley

From Harry **to** Charley

12 January 20:02 GMT

Dear slick, game-winning whatever

MVP? OK. You're right. I'll never get MVP for
lacrosse. Or football. Or rugby. Or cricket. Or
any game that doesn't have a screen, but how
many elite gaming prestiges using QUICK SCOPE
have you got on World of Zombies? One? Two?
HA! I've got three! And that's after only THREE
weeks of playing, which I'm guessing is THREE
more than you'll ever get in your life. And
BTW – number one? Congratulations. That's
pretty cool. I mean it. Nobody I know is number
one at sports – except maybe my best friend
Walnut, who HAS to be good at sports because
his dad is like Mr Sports Dad and makes him
train for rugby EVEN when he's throwing up.
Does your dad make you do that? Maybe that's

just a rugby thing. I don't know –
what do you think?

Harry

From Charley **to** Harry
12 January 11:20 PST

I've told you what I think. Stop writing!

From Harry **to** Charley
12 January 19:22 GMT

Sure. No more emails. No problem. Bye.

From Harry **to** Charley
13 January 18:37 GMT

One last thing. Do they give gamer scholarships to go to college? If they do, I'm definitely going. And if they don't, they should. Oh – and you know that thing you asked me to do with the pipe? That's not going to happen cos I'm never gonna smoke cos smokers are idiots and they die young and I've got plenty to do, OK? Sorry.

Harry

PS Don't forget – my gamer tag is 'kid zombie' and my friend Walnut is 'goofykinggrommet', so if you want to get some pwnage by the KINGS of World of Zombies, then let's see what you got.

You can find us online whenever I'm allowed (which is basically on weekends, plus Wednesday nights when I don't get any homework, but not so much for Walnut cos he has no homework but he does have lots of sports practice or surf club or he's down at the Area 51 Top Secret skate park).

From Charley **to** Harry
13 January 21:12 PST

Here's a funny thing. I go online at the w/e and I hit the World of Zombies website to show my little English cousin how we roll out here in the Sunshine State and I hear this kid called KID ZOMBIE (that's you, right?)

getting beaten on by some dork called
IAMGOD. What's that all about?

Charley

From Harry **to** Charley
14 January 08:03 GMT

Iamgod is a bully and I hate him.

From Charley **to** Harry
14 January 07: 58 PST

So what are you going to do about him?

From Harry **to** Charley
14 January 16:48 GMT

Nothing.

From Charley **to** Harry
14 January 19:10 PST

So how are you gonna get seven elite gaming prestiges, if you do nothin'????

From Harry **to** Charley
15 January 08:00 GMT

Maybe he'll get bored and go and bully somebody else.

From Charley **to** Harry
15 January 07:54 PST

What if he doesn't?

_____

From Harry **to** Charley
15 January 16:03 GMT

Then I don't know.

_____

From Charley **to** Harry
15 January 08:04 PST

I don't know is not an option, Harry.

_____

From Harry **to** Charley
15 January 16:04 GMT

Is for me.

_____

From Charley **to** Harry
15 January 08:07 PST

If this kid's bullying you – you gotta step up.

_____

From Harry **to** Charley
15 January 16:08 GMT

How? The kid is really scary.

_____

From Charley **to** Harry
15 January 08:09 PST

Not if you open a
can of Wuppass.

From Harry **to** Charley
15 January 16:09 GMT

I don't have a can of Wuppass.

From Charley **to** Harry
15 January 17:32 PST

Then that's why you gotta come to your
game-winning, MVP cousin, cos I got cases of
Wuppass. But if you want some, you gotta ask.

From Harry **to** Charley
16 January 07:59 GMT

OK. Can I have a can of Wuppass, please?

_____

From Charley **to** Harry
16 January 08:03 PST

How many you need?

_____

From Harry **to** Charley
16 January 16:13 GMT

I don't know.

_____

From Charley **to** Harry

16 January 18:31 PST

Then let's find out. When's this guy play?

_____

From Harry **to** Charley

17 January 07:58 GMT

Maybe in the evenings?

_____

From Charley **to** Harry

17 January 19:14 PST

So let's take him out this weekend.

CHAPTER TWO

WUPPASS

18 January 20:21 GMT

 Kid Zombie: Hi, everybody! I don't know who is going to read this, or if there is any point in complaining, but basically there's a guy on our site called Iamgod who is a real troll and a bully. Does anybody know what I'm talking about? GB2M soon.

 Goofykinggrommet: Harry? You'd better be careful what you post.

 Kid Zombie: Why? He's a bul–

Iamgod: YO! Did you just call me a TROLL?

 Kid Zombie: Oh. Hi, Iamgod!!

 Iamgod: You are DEAD!!! You hear me, you sick little—

 Mvpguy: Iamgod? You are about to be Iamgone.

 Iamgod: Who's THIS?

 Mvpguy: This is the guy who's telling you to pick on someone your own size. You're not God, you're pathetic. And you're a bully! And if you don't crawl back into your dark stinking pit and stay off WOZ, I'm gonna wup your ass.

Iamgod: You can't make me LEAVE!!!!

 Mvpguy: Yeah? You wanna get banned???? I can ban you.

 Iamgod: You can't BAN me!!!!

 Mvpguy: Oh yeah? Watch. Oh look – I've just given you a 9,999-year ban!!! Like... there! How you like them apples, MR IAMGONE?

 Kid Zombie: Did you just ban Iamgod?

 Mvpguy: From any console. Anywhere. For like the next 9,999 years!!!

Kid Zombie: How did you do that?

 Mvpguy: Like I told you – I opened some Wuppass.

 Kid Zombie: But only game moderators have got Wuppass.

 Mvpguy: Or FRIENDS of game moderators – right, Foxblood 24?

 Foxblood 24: Indeed!

 Mvpguy: There you go, Harry! You kids are free 2 game!

Kid Zombie: That was AWESOME!!! Thank you!!!

 Mvpguy: So next time you need some help - what are you going to do?

 Kid Zombie: Ask for help?

 Mvpguy: Now you're learning!

CHAPTER THREE
THE QUEEN

HIS ROYAL HARRINESS

Tresinkum Farm
Cornwall PL36 0BH
20th January

Her Majesty the Queen
Buckingham Palace
London SW1 1AA

Your Majesty, hi there

My name is Harry Riddles and I don't normally
do this kind of thing, but I think we might need
some help. That's why I'm writing to you. I live
on a farm in Cornwall with my family – that's
my mum, my dad, my elder sister Charlotte and
our dog, Dingbat.

My dog's a mongrel and he's pretty hilarious

– as long as you don't let him off the lead, then he can be like a real pain in the ass (no offence), especially if he sees RABBITS. And if he does see a rabbit, then he'll chase it down a hole and then you'll probably end up having to get a shovel to dig him out, which can take you like hours and hours, but that's what he likes to do so we put up with it.

Anyway, my house is a nice house. In fact, I never want to leave it, but here's the thing, my sister says if somebody doesn't buy my dad's movie soon, we're going to be in big trouble and might even have to find somewhere new to live.

I hope that's not going to happen, but I don't know so that's why I thought I'd write to you. My history teacher, Mr Grigson, said you have like this really big house at Buckingham Palace

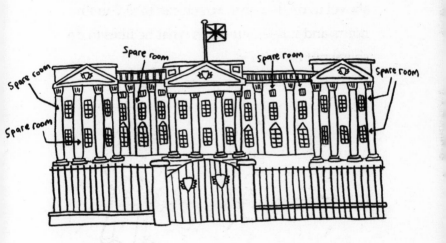

with lots and lots of spare rooms now that all your family have moved out, which made me think you might get kind of lonely living there on your own, like my gran gets kind of lonely. She lives near Swindon and she's always saying how much she wishes we'd come and live with her and I would write to her, but my dad hates Swindon. In fact, my dad doesn't want to leave Cornwall, but if a push came to a shove, I'll bet I could persuade him to give Buckingham Palace a try. So will you think about it? We're nice people. Even my sister, who is almost sixteen, but with any luck she'll be emigrating to Australia soon, so you won't need to worry about her. And as long as you don't have any pet rabbits, my dog is a great dog. Thanks a lot. That's all I have to say.

Good luck and have fun.

Harry Riddles

From Harry **to** Charley
29 January 17:46 GMT

Cuz –

You were right. Asking for help is a good thing.
I just wrote to our queen and guess what? She
wrote back (well, not her, but somebody who
works for her), which was kind of cool and made
our postman wonder what the hell was going on
with the Riddles family that they got a letter in
the post from Buckingham Palace with a royal
seal on it and everything. But that made me
think that if the Queen is that cool, then I'm
gonna keep writing. So thanks for that tip. That
really helped me a lot.

Harry

BTW – in case you're interested, she said we
can't come and live with her.

From Charley **to** Harry
29 January 21:32 PST

The Queen never wrote u back.

From Harry **to** Charley
30 January 16:56 GMT

Did too. And you know something else that just
happened to me that was really cool? I met a
nice girl.

From Charley **to** Harry

30 January 21:03 PST

Wow, that's incredible, Harry! I didn't know they had girls in the boonies.

From Harry **to** Charley

31 January 17:23 GMT

She's not in the boonies (wherever that is), she's in my school and her name is Jessica and this term is her first term and I saw her for like the first time at assembly yesterday morning when she was standing behind me singing my favourite hymn, 'Jerusalem'.

From Charley **to** Harry
31 January 20:04 PST

So how did you see her if she was standing behind you?

From Harry **to** Charley
01 February 09:11 GMT

At first I didn't. At first I heard her cos she had like this really beautiful voice which was great to hear cos normally all I hear is Ed Bigstock standing behind me, shouting in my ear to let me know how deep his voice is, so when I heard her I turned and there she was and I was like OMG – not only can you sing like a bird, but you're really beautiful too. And you know what – she saw me looking and gave me this really nice smile. But then Ed Bigstock kicked me hard cos I guess he likes her too.

From Charley **to** Harry
01 February 01:12 PST

Have you talked to her?

From Harry **to** Charley
01 February 09:12 GMT

No.

From Charley **to** Harry
01 February 01:14 PST

Why not?

From Harry **to** Charley
01 February 09:29 GMT

She's not in my class. Plus, I think she likes drama. Plus, Ed Bigstock came up to me and told me to forget talking to her cos she likes horses and outdoors stuff, not zombies and video games. So really there's no point, is there?

From Charley **to** Harry
01 February 11:32 PST

You're not going to talk to her cos of Ed
Bigstock?

From Harry **to** Charley
01 February 21:04 GMT

Yeah.

From Charley **to** Harry
01 February 22:17 PST

You know what I'd do? If she likes drama, I'd
do drama with her.

From Harry **to** Charley
02 February 09:35 GMT

I hate drama. I like gaming.

From Charley **to** Harry
02 February 10:18 PST

Do you want to hang out with her?

From Harry **to** Charley
02 February 18:20 GMT

Yeah.

From Charley **to** Harry

02 February 21:42 PST

Then do drama.

CHAPTER FOUR
THE SCARLET PUMPERNICKEL

Hi Cuz –

You won't believe this. We had auditions for our
end-of-year school play, *The Scarlet Pumpernickel*.
And I thought maybe you're right. Maybe this is
like the only way I'm ever going to get to hang out
with this girl. So I go along to the auditions and Ed
Bigstock is the first there and he's like, "What the
hell are you doing here, Harry?" I say, "I've come
to audition." And he's like, "For what? There's no
part in this play for a nerdy geek in the times of
the French Evolution!!" "You mean, REVOLUTION,"
I say. And then I hear this laugh like someone
who's trying not to laugh? So I look round and
I see Jessica, standing next to the piano. She'd
been watching us. So Ed says, "Of course I meant

revolution, you idiot." And he's just about to push me when Mr Forbes climbs up the stairs on to the stage. "Harry," he says, "Thank god you're here. Just the man we need!"

Well, I can see Ed is about to blow a fuse because this is not going his way, but then Mr Forbes explains that he thinks I'm the perfect guy to get the lighting and sound rigs up and running because they are like so glitchy and I'm the computer kid. I say, "I don't know if I really want to do sound and lighting to be honest." And that's when Jessica walks over, puts her hand on my shoulder and says, "Wow, do you know how to do that stuff? It would be so brilliant if you could do that, Harry!" Well then I'm like, "If you're asking me, I can definitely give it a try, Jessica."

So, now I'm doing the lighting and the sound for the school play – just like you said I should, which is going to get in the way of my gaming, but I guess sometimes you gotta make tough choices, right?

Harry

From Charley **to** Harry
05 February 21:18 PST

You do if you want a girlfriend.

From Harry **to** Charley
06 February 18:38 GMT

That's kind of what Charlotte said. Actually

what she said was, "Are you in love, you little loser?" She knows I'd prefer to game at home on Wednesdays after school, rather than sit up in the lighting box. So I lied. I said, "Don't be so ridiculous. Of course I'm not in love. I'm way too young. I'm just helping out Mr Forbes before he burns the school down." I don't think she believed me.

Harry

From Harry **to** Harry Styles
Subject: My sister
06 February 21:22 GMT

Harry Styles of One Direction, hi

First off, I know you're in the biggest boy band on the planet and I bet you get a LOT of girls writing to you wanting your autograph and stuff, but you're probably the only guy apart from R-Patz, who can help me stop my sister dating Spencer, who is, no offence, an idiot.

Like you, Spencer is a musician. He works in the music department at my school, but I don't know how he got that job cos he really sucks at playing the piano. My dad calls him the Living Dead, or LD, cos he never talks, he just grins. Even when he's messing everything up, Spencer's always grinning.

Take last week. We had this school singing competition and Ed Bigstock was trying to impress all the girls with his fake, warbly, deep voice by singing that English rugby song, 'Swing Low, Sweet Chariot', but Spencer kept messing with the tempo on the piano, which made Ed sing it slow, then fast, then slow again. It was

really funny, but Ed got so mad he nearly rugby tackled Spencer. My sister thought Spencer had done it on purpose, so she was pleased because she likes bad boys. But I think if there was a choice between you and Spencer, she'd definitely go for you, cos you can probably afford to fill up your own car with petrol and he can't. Plus, if you liked her, maybe you could take her on your world tour for like the next two years? Will you think about it? Great! Thanks a lot!

BTW – you probably want to know if my sister is good-looking. My mum says she's better looking than ANY girl in the whole of Cornwall. But my mum also says I play football like Lionel Messi, so either my mum needs glasses or she's a good liar. So GBTM soon and if Ed Bigstock ever says your band SUCKS again, I will tell him you guys definitely don't suck – unless you don't write back. In which case, I'll just let him say what he wants.

Good luck and have fun.

Harry Riddles

CHAPTER FIVE
EMINEM'S FRIEND

12 February 20:17 GMT

Dear Sir Nicholas Robert Hytner, Director of the National Theatre, hi –

My school is doing this end-of-year play called *The Scarlet Pumpernickel*, and I was hoping maybe you might be able to help me out.

Our play is based on the book, *The Scarlet Pimpernel*, which I'm sure you've read but if you haven't, it's set during the French Revolution, at the time of the Reign of Terror, when the French were hanging all their rich aristocrats because the poor people really had had enough of 'em. But our play is WAY funnier than the book because our teacher, Mr Forbes, wrote it. Plus, we have Ed Bigstock playing the dimwit hero, Sir Percy

Blakeney, and since Ed's two slices short of a sandwich it's no great stretch for him to play an idiot.

Also, we have a great young actor called Jessica, who will play his wife, the beautiful Marguerite St Just. My question for you is: what are our chances of getting our school play on to your stage at the National Theatre?

Today in rehearsals Jessica told Mr Forbes her big dream is to appear in London and be a great actress like Angelina Jolie or Anne Hathaway.

That made me think if you can help me get the Pumpernickel into your place, her big dream would come true. So how do we do that?

Good luck and have fun.

Harry Riddles

BEATS BY DR DRE
CONTACT US

ABOUT YOU

FIRST NAME*
Harry
LAST NAME*
Riddles
EMAIL*
harryriddles1@gmail.com
COUNTRY*
United Kingdom

HOW CAN WE HELP YOU?

SUBJECT*
BUSINESS/PROMOTIONAL ENQUIRY
PRODUCT*
PLEASE SELECT AN ITEM UNDER SPEAKERS

MESSAGE*

Dear Dre Beats

Ed Bigstock broke three of our school speakers
today doing a stupid front flip off the stage
during rehearsals for our school play. I can
probably fix one of 'em but that kid is an ox
and the other two have had it. Would you guys
sponsor our play with a couple of brand-new
speakers? My sister and Spencer say you make
the best stuff out there and if you did want
to help, I could easily keep the speakers in my
room when the play finishes cos I don't have any
speakers of my own and my sister would be really
jealous. Can you do that for me? Great! Thanks!

Good luck and have fun.

Harry Riddles

SUBJECT: Free Product Request
RESPONSE VIA EMAIL (VANESSA)
25 February 10:19 GMT

Dear Mr Riddles,

Thank you for contacting Beats by Dr Dre Support.

My name is Vanessa and I'll be assisting you.

We truly appreciate your enthusiasm for Beats
products, however we are not able to fulfill your
request at this time.

Kind regards,
Vanessa Zurn
Beats by Dr Dre™ Support
Monday – Friday: 7:00am – 8:00pm GMT

Hi Vanessa

Well, that kinda sucks, but maybe we won't need those speakers after all, cos I've been to a few rehearsals now and Ed Bigstock can't say one word without shouting it, so if we did have your Monster Logo Speakers, we'd probably deafen half the audience, which is really not so cool. So thanks for writing back and if Dr Dre is over in England and he wants to come and see a really cool play, can you give him my email and I will definitely get him in? Thanks a lot.

Good luck and have fun.

Harry

Guess who I invited to the school play?
Harry

Who?
Walnut

Dr Dre – Eminem's friend!

Is he coming? That would be
soooo cool.

He hasn't got back to me yet, but you
never know, right?

From Harry **to** Sam Mendes
26 February 20:11 GMT

Sam Mendes, hi there

As the director of James Bond in *Skyfall*, I
think you're probably the only guy who can
knock some sense into my drama teacher Mr
Forbes about the casting for our end-of-term
school play, *The Scarlet Pumpernickel*. Our play
is basically great, but the only problem is Ed
Bigstock, who plays the role of the Pumpernickel.

If the name Bigstock rings a bell, you'll probably
understand where I'm coming from. His dad is the
world-famous polar explorer, Lord Ned Bigstock.
And all his ancestors were also world-famous
explorers, who died up on cold mountains or
alone on the polar caps with their dogs – so this

family is like really great at being alone and also at shouting, but not so great at acting.

The fact Ed happens to be the best-looking kid in my school, the captain of every sports team, and probably the most popular boy the school has ever known has forced Mr Forbes into casting him in the star role, because Mr Forbes understands STAR POWER. But between you and me, Ed really blows, and there's a good chance he could end up putting my friend Jessica in a wheelchair if Mr Forbes lets Ed put any more action scenes into the play to disguise the

fact that he totally sucks at acting and can never remember his lines.

That's why I thought I'd write to you. How did you handle Daniel Craig when he wanted to jump from train to train? Did you let him? Or did you say, "Stop being dumb, we have BLUE SCREENS." Well, we don't have blue screens or computer-generated imagery, we just have Ed Bigstock determined to show off. Please write back to me with your advice. And if you're down on Dartmoor and you want to drop by and watch rehearsals, I'm sure Mr Forbes would really like to meet you and if you know Dr Dre – he might show up too.

Good luck and have fun.

Harry Riddles

Good news! Invited Sam Mendes too.
Harry

To the play?
Walnut

Yeah. Maybe I should invite the Queen.
What do you think?

I doubt she'd come. But why not
try Kelly Slater?

Who?

He's like the best surfer EVER.

Does he like school plays?

I dunno. Try him. (And if he comes, can I come too?)

My guest list is getting a little long but I'll see what I can do.

From Harry **to** Daniel Craig
Subject: Ed Bigstock
27 February 20:57 GMT

Dear Daniel Craig, my mum's most favourite
movie star and the greatest James Bond ever, hi

There's this kid in my school called Ed Bigstock
and I don't know what happened to him over the
school holidays, but he's come back to school
and he now thinks he's like the eleven-year-old
equivalent of you – an ACTION HERO.

But if you've got my job and you have to light
him wherever he goes in our school play, he's
a nightmare to follow because the kid takes a
different route through the audience every time
we rehearse the big chase scene where Ed has
to escape the French soldiers by showing off his

parkour skills and leaping over matron in the front row without taking her teeth out.

I've tried asking him why he takes a different route every time but he just ignores me. However, if YOU wrote to him and told him he needs to start being a professional and stop putting the play at risk, then I bet he'd stop. (But if you did write to him, he'd be impossible to talk to and would probably think you're gonna be his best friend and acting mentor or something – so maybe you should scratch that idea and write to Mr Forbes instead?) Or you could write to me and I could give your letter to him. In fact, that's what you should do. Write to me. And if you want to send me a signed photo, can you please write on it: To Harry's mum, Love Daniel xxxxxxx? She would really, REALLY like that! OK? Thanks a lot!!

Good luck and have fun.

Harry Riddles

BTW – would you like to come to our school play? Let me know quick because if Dr Dre shows

up, he'll have an entourage, cos that guy never goes anywhere without like fifteen people, so we might be a bit tight on chairs.

CHAPTER SIX
BAD MONKEY

H – Why u write H. Styles?
Charlotte

What?
Harry

Mum said u wrote him.

Maybe.

Did he write back?

Not yet.

I thought you didn't like ONE
DIRECTION.

I don't.

So what u write if it wasn't to
say how u a geek fanboy?

2 see if he wanted to take u on his world tour.

If this is one of your stupid games, I'm going to tell Jessica u lve her.

Who told u I lke J?

Everybody at school knows.

That's a lie.

So why are you doing the school play????? BTW – next time you write to Harry, see if he'll lend us some money.

Why?

Ask Dad.

From Harry **to** Charley
01 March 09:33 GMT

Hi Cuz –

Guess what? My dad's bummed cos his film producer partner Alison Hardman couldn't get him any money to buy his movie script and he says it's all her fault that his new movie, *Bad Monkey*, is not going to be in the cinemas but is going straight to DVD. That means now it looks like we won't be able to come out and see you guys this summer cos we're broke, which really sucks.

The good news is, I thought maybe I could help my family and make my OWN movie and then like sell it to CBBC or somebody. So that's what I'm gonna do. I'm gonna make a movie, then I can pay for everybody to fly out to California.

Harry

––––––––––––

From Charley **to** Harry
01 March 11:25 PST

You, make a movie? HA!

––––––––––––

From Harry **to** Charley
01 March 19:28 GMT

My dad says this is what artists always come up against. Negativity. But I'll show you.

––––––––––––

From Charley **to** Harry
01 March 11:30 PST

Yeah? So what are you going to write about?

From Harry **to** Charley
01 March 19:40 GMT

Zombies.

From Charley **to** Harry
01 March 11:40 PST

You're gonna make a zombie movie?

From Harry **to** Charley
01 March 11:25 GMT

In stop-motion. With this app I bought for like 60p.

_____

From Charley **to** Harry
01 March 13:02 PST

Show it to me in like five years when you've finished animating it.

_____

From Harry **to** Charley
01 March 21:06 GMT

It's not gonna take five years to animate if I get my friends to help me.

From Charley **to** Harry
01 March 18:30 PST

What friends? You live online.

From Harry **to** Charley
02 March 11:25 GMT

I've got plenty of friends. Like my friend Walnut.
He kicks butt at surfing, so he's not a geek.
In fact, he came fourth in a competition at
Newquay last week.

From Charley **to** Harry
02 March 10:42 PST

Well, that's one kid. So I look forward to seeing it
in about two and a half years, then.

From Harry **to** Charley
02 March 18:50 GMT

It won't take me that long. You watch...

From Harry **to** Dad
03 March 20:25 GMT

Pups,

I can never find you cos you are always out in
your office working, or out walking the dog, so
I thought maybe I could mail you. Here's what's
going on. I think you and me need to make a
really cool ZOMBIE film (like an animation?),
which we could then SELL to TV and get this
family out of TROUBLE.

When I told Mum this was my plan, she thought
basically it was sweet, but I don't think she heard
me cos zombie films aren't sweet, are they?
And besides, she was trying to fix the washing
machine, so I don't think she was really listening.
So I told it to her again and she said, "Why does

it have to be a zombie movie, Harry? Why not a little doggie movie? Or one with farm animals?" I told her all that stuff is boring. Plus, nobody has made a kids' show with ZOMBIES!!! Mum said, "Are you surprised?" Then she told me I should take the dog for a walk cos I'm an Internet addict and I need to get more exercise or I'm going to turn into a goggle-eyed MONSTER like this guy:

I told Mum all kids like me who live out in the country are bored out of their tree, which is why we live online and walking the dog is not going to change anything. Besides, that dog gets enough exercise anyway cos he's always out with you.

Anyway, then Charlotte comes in and she starts saying all this stuff about how we've got terrible money problems and I should be getting my head round moving to a new school, not trying to make a stupid zombie movie. Charlotte said if I wanted to write stupid movies that never make money, you and me would make a great team.

Well, then Mum got angry with Charlotte and told her to be more respectful to you and that everything was going to be fine, and Charlotte laughed like the evil witch she is and said we're all a bunch of ostriches, with our heads deep in the sand, cos everything is definitely NOT going to be fine.

You know what I think? I think the sooner Charlotte leaves home, the better off we'll all be. So will you help me make my movie? **PLEASE?** And if you have time, see how much a ticket to Australia costs.

Harry

From Dad **to** Harry
Subject: Your movie
03 March 22:54 GMT

My kid,

We could definitely do a little home movie and stick it up on YouTube – if that's what you want to do.

Pups xx

From Harry **to** Dad
04 March 17:24 GMT

Pups,

Who makes money out of YouTube? Walnut's uploaded a ton of stuff his dad took of him surfing and he's never made a penny (and that's when the surf is like HUMONGOUS). So that's why I was thinking we should get it up on CBBC or, if they don't pay well, then Fox, because I need to make some MONEY so we can go and see our cousins.

Harry

From Dad **to** Harry
04 March 21:45

OK. What's the title and what's your story?

I think it's gonna be called *My Pet Zombie* and
it's about this bored kid who finds this little
baby zombie. And maybe the reason he finds
this zombie is his mum doesn't want him playing
video games again (yawn). So she sends the kid
out the house to walk the dog and THAT'S when
he finds the ZOMBIE. Hiding in the hedge or
down a rabbit hole or something? And maybe
the little zombie is like really sick, just like E.T.
was really sick? So the kid rescues the baby
zombie and brings him home to look after him,
but he can't take him in the house to live with
them cos his mum'll tell him there's no room in
the house for more pets. So the kid has to hide
the zombie out in the hay barn. And this is where
the story gets basically hilarious, because Farmer

Harold thinks the zombie is here to EAT all his chickens, but the kid tells him the zombie isn't a FLESH-EATING zombie – he only eats carrots! And that's the end of my first show. Good twist, huh?

Harry

From Dad **to** Harry
05 March 20:33 GMT

Little man,

Are you sure about this? Vegetarian zombies aren't that scary – unless, of course, you're a carrot.

Or, a potato.

Pups xx

From Harry **to** Dad
05 March 20:47 GMT

Pups,

Not scary? OK. Then how come Ed Bigstock
accidentally on purpose broke my claymation
zombie model in my art class today? Him and
Jackie Chan were like, "Oh my god, that's so sick,
Harry!" Then he knocked it over!!! Unless, of
course, they were jealous that I was going to win
the end-of-term art competition because Ed's art
looks like a car crash (if u're being nice).

Anyway, I thought you always said to me we need
to find new ways of telling old stories. Well, this
is new. I mean, how many vegetarian zombie
stories have you ever seen? Plus, basically, it
would give you a JOB and Mum says you're going

to need one soon.

Harry xxxx

From Dad **to** Harry

Subject: Unemployment

05 March 21:38 GMT

My kid,

If you really want a vegetarian zombie, why don't
you do some drawings of the main characters and
the farmhouse, barn and farmyard where all the
action takes place. Then email them to me and we
can write a script. And as for a job, don't worry, I
told your mother I got a few exciting opportunities
I'm considering, so stop worrying and GO TO BED!

Pups xx

From Harry **to** Dad
05 March 21:41 GMT

I'm going to bed, but what about you? Shouldn't
you go to bed, too?

From Dad **to** Harry
05 March 22:47 GMT

I'm working.

From Harry **to** David O. Russell
6 March 20:19 GMT

Dear David O. Russell, BAFTA-winning film director, hi

My dad is one of your biggest fans and he thinks all your movies are pretty great. Like you, my dad is a screenwriter, but unlike you he's having problems getting his stuff into the cinemas and my mum is worried that he's losing his confidence, which has never happened to him before.

What do you do if your movie goes straight to DVD? That just happened to my dad and he's been doing this for a long, long time, but he's having a bad run and I don't know how to help him. What do you think I should do?

BTW – have you ever made a zombie film? Are you planning on making a zombie film? If so, please don't make it about a kid who makes friends with a vegetarian zombie who is really sick, cos that's my idea. OK? Thanks a lot!

Good luck and have fun.

Harry Riddles

From Harry **to** Dad

7 March 23:35 GMT

Pups –

My sketches – what do you think?

Worried chickens

DEAD Carrot

Setting:

Farm House

Hay barn

Farmer Harold

CHAPTER SEVEN
A ZOMBIE NAMED SPENCER

HIS ROYAL HARRINESS

Tresinkum Farm
Cornwall PL36 OBH
8th March

Mr David Cameron
The Prime Minister
10 Downing Street
London SW1A 2AA

Mr David Cameron, Prime Minister, hi there

Has this ever happened to you? I got home
from my school yesterday and this bailiff
was at my house trying to tell my mum he
should be allowed to take my Xbox and our TV
because my dad didn't pay some bill – which
was like really SCARY. Luckily, my dad gave

him this old car we had sitting in our field, so things weren't a complete disaster, but they nearly were and that's why I'm writing to you.

Some kids in my school told me you and your family like to come to Cornwall for your summer holidays. Here's a great idea. Why don't you rent OUR house in August? We have this really nice little house, IN CORNWALL, and it's near the sea. Plus, if you did want to rent our house, my dad could pay the bills on time and my Xbox would be safe.

I haven't told my mum about this, but I think it could be a really good idea as long as you don't mind walking our dog. His name is Dingbat and he likes to get stuck down rabbit holes and chase cows, which can be pretty annoying, but he's a really nice dog and I think you'll like him (but don't let him on the beds cos he's always muddy and my mum really hates having to change the sheets more than once a week). Will you think about it? Please? Thanks a lot!

Good luck and have fun.

Harry Riddles

From Harry **to** Alison Hardman
Subject: *My Pet Zombie*
11 March 20:06 GMT

Hi Alison Hardman,

First off, congratulations for the movie you made
with my dad, *Bad Monkey*, it was like totally
hilarious and THANK GOD the movie went
straight to DVD. Honestly. If you guys had made a
movie for the cinemas, there's no way I could've
seen that movie for another year cos the woman
who runs our local cinema won't let me watch
12A movies unless we're accompanied by an
ADULT, which means me and Walnut always
have to go to the cinema with my mum. And my
mum won't sit in our local cinema unless there's
absolutely nothing else for us to do, because she
says the place really stinks of cow MANURE. She

says all the young farmers who come to watch movies round where we live don't like to change out of their work boots after a day on the farm, so the cinema HONKS!!! But she also said if Daniel Craig was in the movie, she'd put up with the smell. I don't know why.

Anyway, I hope you guys make a sequel, and if you do maybe you should think about putting Daniel Craig in it, cos then you'll definitely sell like three tickets. So good luck with that idea.

Do you guys make TV shows? I have this really cool TV show you should help me make. It's called *My Pet Zombie* and if you like *Shaun the Sheep* or any of those stop-motion shows, this is like one zillion times better cos IT'S GOT ZOMBIES!!!

But I can't make this show on my own. I'm gonna need a bunch of model-makers to help me make all my characters do all the things they have to do, which is a LOT OF THINGS, or it will take me like five years and that's way too long to wait to visit my cousins. So that made me think if I could hire some kids from Year 6, I could get this thing done in no time. And that's where you guys could help. Boarders in Year 6 get like 50p EVERY Wednesday to spend on sweets – which means by Tuesday night they'll sell their best friend for a Mars bar.

I'm serious. If I gave Jackie Chan three Twix bars to help out in the art room after school, that kid would work all night long making me my claymation models, and so what if he fell asleep the next day in science? He's a genius. He can afford to sleep through that class cos he gets straight As anyway.

But we're gonna need chocolate. I don't mean like ten or twenty bars, I'm talking like 35 bars a week, minimum. So if you want to send me money, I can definitely get my dad to stop off at the newsagent's on the way into school. But we need to get moving quickly or we

will not get this made before the end of term,
OK? Thanks a lot.

Good luck and have fun.

Harry Riddles

From Harry **to** Alison Hardman
Subject: *My Pet Zombie*
18 March 20:22 GMT

Hi Alison –

OK. I know you guys are really busy with all the movies you are trying to make and to be honest I'm up to my ears with rehearsing our school play, which is gonna be really great, BTW – and if you did want to come and see it, I don't know if I can get you any free tickets any more cos I'm waiting to hear back from Daniel Craig, Dr Dre and Sam Mendes, and if they come I don't know if Mr Forbes will allow me to invite anybody else. But I can definitely try, if you want.

More importantly – what do you think of *My Pet Zombie*? We need to get moving on this before any more boarders are yanked out of Year 6 cos their parents can't pay the school fees – which is happening a LOT by the way. My dad said it's because we're all standing on the edge of a FISCAL CLIFF and we're only one step away from financial ruin – which is why I thought I better write to you again before we all fall off that stupid cliff.

You probably need to know more about my show. I can send you the whole idea but here's the basics. If you've ever played World of Zombies, you'll know where I'm coming from. *My Pet Zombie* takes place in the future, but after a nuclear attack when pretty much all of England has turned into a nation full of zombies except for this one place: CORNWALL! YAY!

So my story starts when this kid is down at the River Tamar. (You know the river that's like the boundary between Cornwall and Devon? That one.) And he sees this old pram wash up on the shore. (And if you're thinking this bit is like something out of RE – that's exactly where I stole it from.) So the kid thinks: *What's in that pram, I wonder?* The kid goes over, finds this sweet little baby zombie, but this little zombie is really SICK!!!

So the kid picks up the zombie, puts him in his backpack and takes him home to his farm. But he doesn't know what to call him. Then he has a brilliant idea. He calls the zombie Spencer. After my sister's boyfriend. And that's my first episode – 'A Zombie Named Spencer'.

But I'm totally open to any story ideas you have. Get back to me soon and let's start making it.

Good luck and have fun.

Harry Riddles

From Phoebe **to** Harry
Subject: My Pet Zombie
24 March 09:52 GMT

Hi Harry,

Alison is on location, so she asked me to get in touch with you on her behalf and thank you for your kind words about *Bad Monkey*. It was a bitter pill to swallow, not securing a theatrical release, but as you say, at least it made it to DVD.

Unfortunately, we are not currently in the television business, being a film company, but thank you very much for considering us. My *Pet Zombie* is a very interesting project and we hope you and your father will have a great deal of success with it on the Internet. However, we would not feel comfortable employing school children, outside of union rules and regulations, and having them work for less than the minimum wage, so we will not be sending you any money for chocolate bars. But if there's anything more we can do to help, please do not hesitate to ask.

Good luck and have fun to you too.

Phoebe Cakes (Assistant to Alison Hardman)

From Harry **to** Phoebe
Subject: Bitter pills.
24 March 18:34 GMT

Hi Phoebe,

I don't know how much luck or fun I'm going to have if I can't pay the kids in Year 6 to make my TV show, but if you guys don't want to help me make *My Pet Zombie* and you want to keep making movies that go straight to DVD, I think you might be making a BIG mistake cos my dad says TV is the FUTURE and the film business is DEAD unless you are the big guys with like 200 million to spend on Marvel comic books (which you definitely are NOT).

FYI – no one pays to watch stuff on the Internet cos everything is free or stolen. And this TV show is all about MAKING MONEY and moving off that fiscal cliff and going out to see my cousins in California.

So good luck again and I hope you can have fun, but it doesn't sound to me like you're having a lot of fun if everything you make ends up in the DVD bin at SuperSave.

Harry

From Harry **to** Charley

25 March 16:12 GMT

Hey Cuz –

Boy, am I dumb. Today I'm standing in the yard
and I see Jessica and she comes over and we're
just about to have our first conversation, when
Ed Bigstock suddenly runs up and starts shouting
that she and him will both be in Scotland in
August and they should hang out and go fishing
together. When Jessica had taken her hands away
from her ears, she looked a bit surprised and
disappointed, but she sort of smiled and said,
"Sure, why not?", then she asked me if I liked
fishing. I said, "If you mean hacking credit card
numbers, I haven't tried it." It was a stupid joke,
but nobody got it. So then Ed says, "See, that's all
he thinks about! Stupid computers! IDIOT!"

———————————————

From Charley **to** Harry
25 March 08:17 PST

Why are you asking about hacking credit card numbers?

From Harry **to** Charley
25 March 16:21 GMT

Phishing. Come on, you gotta know what that means, right? Anyway, guess what Ed's hoping to do this summer when he's not fishing? He wants to climb Mont Blanc with his dad and probably jump off it in a flying suit. That kid has definitely got a screw loose.

CHAPTER EIGHT
DRAGONS' DEN

From Harry **to** Dad
Subject: The *Dragons' Den* TV show
26 March 20:51 GMT

Pups,

I know in your business everybody works for free and hopes one day they'll get paid when their stuff is finally made, but nobody in my school will work that way. I've tried but these kids want cash up front – which is not in the spirit of the arts, but what can I do?

Anyway, I was thinking if I want to get *My Pet Zombie* made, what you and me need to do is find somebody who will give us some money so I can buy the chocolate and then pay the kids in Year 6 and then they will stop moaning and start helping me. So I saw this show on TV called *Dragons' Den* and I think maybe this is the perfect solution for us. You know the one I'm talking about? A bunch of millionaire businessmen who want to find business projects that'll make 'em zillionaires?

So anyway I downloaded this application form. Can you see if there's stuff in it I should change before we send it in?

Love you, Dad.

Harry

DRAGONS' DEN APPLICATION FORM

NAME:
Harry Riddles

AGE:
10.3

HOME:
Tresinkum Farm, Cornwall

WORK:
Sure – what have you got in mind?

MOBILE:
My parents told me not to give out that number.

EMAIL:
harryriddles1@gmail.com

COMPANY ADDRESS (if relevant):
My bedroom.

PRESENT OCCUPATION:
Bored.

MARITAL STATUS:
At my age? NO!

PREVIOUS JOBS (please list):
1) Car washer for my dad.
2) Egg seller of Farmer Harold's best Cornish eggs.
3) Potato seller (if the rain hasn't ruined them).

BUSINESS:
In a perfect world? Killing zombies.

NAME OF BUSINESS:
Pet Zombie Productions.

DESCRIBE YOUR IDEA IN ONE LINE:

An animated kids' TV show about a young boy
and his best friend, a VEGETARIAN ZOMBIE!!!!

AMOUNT OF INVESTMENT REQUIRED:

35 bars of chocolate a week for four weeks. Maybe
more.

% SHARE IN EXCHANGE:

Share of what? All the chocolate is going to be
eaten by the kids in Year 6.

EXECUTIVE SUMMARY:

**(In the Executive Summary, you have the
chance to sell yourself and your idea, and give
a clear and comprehensive outline of your
business or product. What problem does your
idea solve? What stage are you at with patent or
copyright protection? Where are you up to with
prototyping or testing? Describe sales, if your**

business is trading. Please supply any additional information you feel may be useful.)

I don't understand what you're asking, so let's skip that bit. Instead let me tell you about the problem my idea solves. What do kids like me watch before *The Simpsons*? Every night I come home from my school and there's NOTHING on TV until 6.30. Where's the show that stops me wanting to go up into my den and start GAMING? Where's THAT show at six in the evening? 30 minutes later when *The Simpsons* comes on – that's where that show is. So *My Pet Zombie* solves that problem and gives kids like me what we want to see when we need to see it – which is when we get home and we're tired and we need to eat like ten Yorkshire puddings before we go completely crazy and start shooting zombies. OK? So that's the problem my show solves.

As for copyright protection? I don't know what that is, but I'll ask my dad.

Where am I with my prototyping? If you mean
have we made a show yet? No. If you mean, do I
know what we're going to do? Yes. All I need to
do is bribe the kids in Year 6 and hope you guys
don't rip me off.

DO YOU HAVE A WRITTEN BUSINESS PLAN?
Yes: 1) Make lots on money. 2) Go to California and
visit our cousins. 3) Stop my mum and dad worrying.

HAVE YOU BEEN ON TELEVISION BEFORE?
Only in this GoPro movie I made with my friends
where we attack my dad in the chicken shed with
Nerf guns, then BLAST HIM to smithereens
– which was good fun, by the way. We totally
nailed him.

DO YOU HAVE ANY CRIMINAL CONVICTIONS?
(Please give details whether spent or otherwise):
I closed my Facebook account before the police

got to me – so I got away with that one, but thanks for reminding me (not).

DO YOU GIVE YOUR PERMISSION FOR THE BBC TO CARRY OUT A FULL CRIMINAL RECORD BUREAU CHECK TO VERIFY THE ABOVE DETAILS?

Here's the thing – I haven't been in trouble cos I'm only like ten, but I know my dad has had a few scrapes. For example: he got arrested in Los Angeles when he was a teenager, probably for being drunk. Plus some place in Florida, a place in Nicaragua, a place in Colombia (that's in South America). I don't think he got arrested anywhere else in South America, but I know he spent a night at the police station near where we live. I don't know why. So maybe he shouldn't come on your show (if that's OK?).

HAVE YOU EVER BEEN BANKRUPT OR

BEEN DISQUALIFIED FROM BEING A DIRECTOR OF A COMPANY?
(Please give details.)

This is my first business, so the answer is no (I think). I did get disqualified once, but that was when we went karting at St Eval and I rammed my sister, who definitely deserved it.

ENTREPRENEUR AVAILIBILITY:
(Recordings are likely to take place in Salford. Should you be successful in being selected for the series, you will be required to attend one recording day, which could be a weekday.)

Can we do it in the school holidays? And maybe Skype would be better than Salford, because I don't think Western Greyhound have a bus line that runs from Cornwall to Salford (wherever that is). OK? Thanks a lot.

From Harry **to** Charley
28 March 16:52 GMT

Guess what? Jessica talked to me without Ed.

_____

From Charley **to** Harry
28 March 18:01 PDT

Oh yeah – what did she say?

_____

From Harry **to** Charley
29 March 09:52 GMT

You're so right.

_____

From Charley **to** Harry
29 March 10:58 PDT

She said, "You're so right"?

From Harry **to** Charley
29 March 20:03 GMT

Yeah.

From Charley **to** Harry
29 March 13:05 PDT

That's it?

From Harry **to** Charley
29 March 20:07 GMT

Yeah.

_____

From Charley **to** Harry
29 March 13:11 PDT

Why did she say that?

_____

From Harry **to** Charley
29 March 20:14 GMT

Because I told Mr Forbes that if he lets Ed go
where he wants when he does his parkour-
through-the-audience thing, I won't be able to
shine a spotlight on Jessica and she needs one,

or she might fall off the stage and break a leg or something when he yells, "JUMP!!!"

From Charley **to** Harry
29 March 13:24 PDT

Did she say anything else?

From Harry **to** Charley
30 March 09:47 BST

No – but that's a start, right?

From Charley **to** Harry
30 March 20:31 PDT

I guess.

CHAPTER NINE
WORSE THAN JUVEY

From Dad **to** Harry
Subject: Your application
01 April 20:42 BST

Mogulman –

OK – before you think of sending them this,
you will need all kinds of other stuff like, A) a
finished script, B) a budget of costs to make all
your shows, C) a storyboard of the first episode,
D) some sample footage of your first episode
and, if possible, a letter of genuine interest from
somebody who will buy it and broadcast it. The
Dragons want to know ALL that before they
even THINK about giving you money. Even for
chocolate.

Then they'll ask you how much you hope to sell it
for. Then they'll want to know how much money

you will give them when you sell it. When you
have all of that, you will be ready for them and
they might – MIGHT – help you. But don't count
on it. By the way – how old do you have to be?

Dad

_____

From Harry **to** Dad
01 April 20:43 BST

Sixteen.

_____

From Dad **to** Harry
01 April 20:50 BST

So how are you going to do that?

_____

From Harry **to** Dad
01 April 20:50 BST

I'm not – YOU are.

From Dad **to** Harry
01 April 20:52 BST

I'm not going to Salford to talk to the Dragons.

From Harry **to** Dad
01 April 20:53 BST

Why not – you haven't got anything else to do.

From Dad **to** Harry
01 April 20:58 BST

What are you talking about? What do you think I do out in my office all day? I work.

DRAFT EMAILS NOT YET SENT

From Harry **to** Dad
01 April 21:01 BST

Mum says work is something you get paid to do.

From Harry **to** Charley
03 April 21:30 BST

OMG, this is like the worst thing that has ever happened to me. My mum just came into my room and I knew something was up, because she didn't tell me to turn off my Xbox, which she'd definitely normally do at 9 on a Wednesday night, so I carried on blasting away and then my mum says to me, "What would you say if you had to move schools next year? Could be fun, right?" I didn't answer. Who would want to

leave my school? My school is great. So she tells me that there's this woman in the village who keeps telling her how great the local school is and how we should all support it because it's people like us who can make a big difference and change the system that keeps turning out people like David Cameron and George Osborne.

I said, "What's wrong with David Cameron? He's a nice guy and he wrote back to me. So what if he doesn't want to rent our house? At least he made the effort to write. Unlike Harry Styles. Or the National Theatre guy. Or Daniel Craig. Or Sam Mendes."

Mum said, "Why would Sam Mendes write to you?" I said, "To accept my invitation to the school play." Mum said, "Did he?" I said, "He hasn't got back to me." My mum didn't know what to say next. So before I had to explain more, I said, "Mum, I don't want to change the system. I like the system. I'm happy at my school. I don't want to leave." But my mum said she had arranged for me to go along for a taster day after the Easter holidays and try our local school, so that's what I gotta do, but you know what happened when I told Ed Bigstock I would not be there for rehearsals because I was going to be spending the day at this new school? He laughed and said his big brother knew a kid who went there and he lasted like one week before he ran away from home and was never seen again. He said the place is worse than juvey. I hope he was exaggerating or I'm going to need to learn some ass-kicking skills pretty quick.

I'm goin' 2 bed now. I've got a headache.

Harry

From Charley **to** Harry
03 April 18:32 PDT

Cuz –

Keep your head down, stay out of trouble, and don't open your mouth, OK? Be cool and not what you are, which is a little geek. Lemme know how it goes.

Charley

CHAPTER TEN
A VISIT TO MORDOR

A VISIT TO MORDOR

(An English creative writing assignment based on
The Hobbit, by Harry W. Riddles)

Today I left my home in the Shire and took the
Western Greyhound bus over to Mordor to visit
this new school my mum and dad told me I might
have to go to. Basically, it's called Mount Doom
School (St Piran's) and to be honest, most prisons
look nicer.

Mount Doom has an open taster day for all
ten-year-old Hoppits who have to move schools
because of this Recession. Taster day means
feeding all the newbie Hoppits (kids like me)
to the dumb trolls (kids in Year 6) gathered at
the Black Gates waiting for someone to grab.
Fortunately, this Hoppit snuck through the Black
Gates without incident and managed to make it all
the way through to lunch before he was mugged in
the orc feeding pen by two greedy female dwarves

from Year 6, who wanted to steal his ice cream and jelly. That was pretty bad, but things got a whole lot WORSE when this Hoppit discovered that the headmaster, Mr Alastair Mevagissey, was not really a headmaster, but was in fact the evil wizard Sauron, AKA The Dark Lord himself. Worse, The Dark Lord was planning on taking over the world soon after school finished at 3.30 that afternoon. What could this Hoppit do? Something awesome? Or would Sauron's wicked spell condemn these poor orc- and dwarf kids to a life of MISERY FOR EVER? (Which probably meant not being able to leave school until they were like 422.)

So the Hoppit called his good friend, Optimus Prime, leader of the Autobots. "Optimus," the little Hoppit said. "We have an emergency and I really, really need your help."

The Hoppit told the Autobot that not only was St Piran's an evil breeding ground of dangerous trolls and greedy dwarves who wanted to take over our world and steal everybody's ice cream, but also that their master, the evil Lord Sauron, AKA Alastair Mevagissey, had stolen the ALLSPARK – which, as we all know, gives him the POWER TO RULE THE UNIVERSE.

"Can you help me save our world and we'll owe you one?" the little Hoppit asked the giant Autobot.

A deal was done and at just after 3.16 that afternoon, Optimus Prime and his fellow Autobots attacked Sauron and his troll army at Mordor. A ferocious battle raged in the dark skies above Mount Doom and the Autobots smoted the trolls and the orcs like a hot knife going through stolen ice cream. When the final bell rung, Sauron was defeated and the wicked spell that had enslaved these poor student kids was BROKEN for ever and happy days returned to St Piran's. YAY!!! And all because of this brave little Hoppit.

With the orc- and dwarf kids free to live like normal kids again (and maybe grow a few more inches in some cases), the Hoppit caught the last bus home from Mordor and returned to the Shire, where he discovered things were getting better by the minute cos his dad had just won the lottery, so he never had to move schools and he never had to leave the Shire and nothing ever changed in his life, which is just the way he LIKED IT. THANK GOD. THE END.

I commend you on your imaginative mash-up of ideas and your obvious love of monsters, Harry. A good effort and I'm sure your new school isn't **that** *bad. Well done.* (B⁺)

World of ZOMBIES
COMMUNITY FORUM

 Kid Zombie: Walnut, the dog ate my headset, can you type?

 Goofykinggrommet: Sure. Where u bin?

 Kid Zombie: St Piran's.

 Goofykinggrommet: You went to St Piran's? How was it? Did they put u in a bin?

Kid Zombie: No.

 Goofykinggrommet: Did you like it?

 Kid Zombie: No.

 Goofykinggrommet: U should come to my school.

 Kid Zombie: I don't want to move schools. I like it where I am.

 Goofykinggrommet: So what's gonna happen?

Kid Zombie: I don't know, but my dad says he's got something really, really exciting starting for him next week, so maybe nothing'll change. I don't know. I hope not.

 Goofykinggrommet: Guess who I met at Area 51?

 Kid Zombie: Who?

 Goofykinggrommet: Ed something? Goes to your school?

 Kid Zombie: Not Ed Bigstock?

 Goofykingrommet: Him.

Kid Zombie: Did you tell him you were my friend?

 Goofykinggrommet: Uh huh.

 Kid Zombie: What did he say?

 Goofykinggrommet: He said you're a gamer geek.

 Kid Zombie: He said that?

 Goofykinggrommet: No actually, what he said was he owned you and basically you were his slave.

 Kid Zombie: He said that?

Goofykinggrommet: Yeah.

 Kid Zombie: That kid is such a loser.

 Goofykinggrommet: But you shoulda seen him skate. He was hilarious.

 Kid Zombie: Why?

 Goofkinggrommet: He sucks!!!!!!

 Kid Zombie: Great!!!!!

 Goofykinggrommet: You know the Wall of Death? Four feet of vert, eight feet of transition? At the back end of the park after the snake run and the big bowl that's like that Dogtown bowl? A sick wall?

Kid Zombie: Kind of.

 Goofykinggrommet: He tried dropping in from the top to show off to this girl.

 Kid Zombie: What girl?

 Goofykinggrommet: Really nice girl. Pretty.

 Kid Zombie: What was her name?

 Goofykinggrommet: Jess something.

 Kid Zombie: Jessica?

Goofykinggrommet: Yeah.

Kid Zombie: OK. So what was Jessica doing at Area 51?

Goofykinggrommet: I dunno. She wasn't skating – she was reading.

Kid Zombie: Reading what?

Goofykinggrommet: Some papers?

Kid Zombie: The school play. But she came with him?

Goofykinggrommet: Yeah.

Kid Zombie: Did she hear what he said about me?

 Goofykinggrommet: She told him to stop being so mean.

 Kid Zombie: OK – so then what happened?

 Goofkinggrommet: He climbs up to the top, tries dropping in and totally eats it before he even gets to the ramp opposite. I thought he'd knocked himself out.

 Kid Zombie: Yeah, well wouldn't have been the first time. The kid's not right in the head.

 Goofykinggrommet: Well, he went straight back up, dropped in again, and this time he didn't even make it past the end of the ramp. He face-planted.

Kid Zombie: That musta hurt!!!!

 Goofykinggrommet: If it did, he didn't show it.

 Kid Zombie: So then what happens? Did he leave?

 Goofykinggrommet: No - he tells this girl, watch this! This time I'm gonna make it!

 Kid Zombie: And?

 Goofykinggrommet: He makes the drop, makes the gap across to the next ramp, but when he hits the ramp opposite, he's totally out of control and he shoots up the ramp, gets launched like ten feet up in the air and he lands upside down on his head. Well this time, everybody in the park thinks he's definitely broken his neck. So we all run over and he's like lying there not moving, but he wasn't dead – he just knocked himself out.

 Kid Zombie: Thank god for that (not).

 Goofykinggrommet: I've never seen anybody like him. He's totally fearless.

 Kid Zombie: That's why his family are polar explorers. They don't feel pain or fear.

 Goofykinggrommet: If he learns how to skate before he kills himself, he's gonna be a great sk8r. My dad's yelling. I gotta go to rugby. See ya.

 Kid Zombie: Wait a minute – did you talk to Jessica about me? Walnut? WALNUT!!!

From Harry **to** Tyson Fury, English heavyweight boxing prospect
01 May 20:32 BST

Tyson Fury, hi there

Me and my dad watched your fight on TV and it was really GREAT. When that guy knocked you down, we thought, *That's it, Tyson Fury has lost*, but you got back on your feet and you won – which just goes to show you should never quit until you're knocked out. My dad said that's what happens if you got courage. Even when things are going against you, you fight back, then you win against all odds. So well done, Tyson Fury. You're an inspiration to the Riddles family.

The reason I'm writing is I might have to move schools next year. And if I do, I'm going to need to learn how to stick up for myself. I'm not saying this new school is like going off to war in Afghanistan, but it's close. And the place I'm at now? It's a really nice school and there's no bullying unless you want to talk about Ed Bigstock, who is kind of a bully, but more really a prize jerk.

Anyway, have you ever thought about teaching kids how to box? I know you're like six feet nine and you weigh eighteen stone and you might look down at someone like me and think, this little shrimp can't BOX, but I'm almost four feet and I'm gonna be eleven pretty soon and I'm not a tough guy, but I need to do something or I'm gonna get my ass kicked big time (which, basically, I don't want).

And if you did want to teach me how to box, I could definitely teach you how to get three (maybe four?) elite gaming prestiges on World of Zombies with quick scope (which is a pretty fair trade by the way cos some kids take like eight months to get that far. Not that you are a kid, no offence).

One other thing (and this is a really great idea, by the way). Why don't you have one of your boxing things down here in Cornwall? If you did, my dad said we could DEFINITELY sell out WADEBRIDGE TOWN HALL. And that would be really cool because then we could come and watch you. Plus, you'd give my dad a job (which he kinda needs).

Keep knocking people out.

Good luck and have fun.

Harry Riddles

CHAPTER ELEVEN
SUPERSAVE

Where are u?
Charlotte

Bus
Harry

Meet me at SuperSave. NOW!!!

Why?

Just get there!

From Harry **to** Charley
03 April 18:21 BST

Hey Cuz –

Guess what? My dad got a job. Yay! The only
problem is he's not writing movies for Hollywood,
but stacking shelves at the SuperSave. Me and
my sister went down to see him this afternoon
and basically he was pretty embarrassed and
tried hiding behind the cheese counter until my
sister said, "We see you, Dad. Stop hiding." So my
dad comes out and my sister unloads on him and
says he's a total fail and my mum should have
married somebody else – which made him pretty
upset, as you can imagine, cos nobody wants to
hear that garbage, especially not from a bratty
daughter. Mind you, if my mum HAD married

somebody else, I might have got a NICER sister. Anyway, my sister went off and I told my dad not to listen to her – she's an evil teenager and my dad's a great dad and he should just put her up for adoption and then we'd all be better off.

My dad said my sister has a point. He does feel like a fail. I said you're not a fail. Working at the SuperSave is a GREAT JOB and we're all really proud of you! Plus, we'll never run out of milk! But I don't think he saw it that way.

Then the manager came over and he told my dad to get back to work, because the cheese counter wasn't a family get-together centre. So I had to leave, but before I went my dad said any minute now things are going to get a LOT BETTER for the Riddles family, which is good news, cos my mum and dad have been arguing a lot about money recently. George Tibbs said his mum and dad really hate each other, but they can't AFFORD to get divorced, which I'm hoping is gonna be the deal with us. I hope we're too poor, because if my dad goes, who's gonna help me with my homework? Plus, I'll really miss him.

Harry

From Harry **to** Bear Grylls
03 May 19:53 BST

Dear Bear Grylls, survival expert and star of *Born Survivor*, hi

My friend Walnut said you might be the guy who could help me survive growing up with my sister. Her name is Charlotte and she is like the human equivalent of a rattlesnake. Worse, maybe.

On your website it says you climbed Mount Everest when you were just 23 years old and it took you over 90 days of extreme weather and limited sleep and running out of oxygen deep inside the 'death zone', which is anywhere above 8,000 metres. Not in my house. The 'death zone' starts at the top of the stairs and includes the bathroom, where my sister has got all her make-up, and also her bedroom. If I go in those areas without her permission, I'm dead, which makes my life pretty impossible as you can imagine.

Then I read that you also had a sister, and that made me wonder – is that why you joined the SAS? Maybe if I specialised in combat survival, demolitions and unarmed combat my sister would think twice before spanking my ass when she's mad. What do you think? I'm guessing I'm too young to join the SAS, but let's say I joined the Scouts – could they teach me how to become a combat survival expert like you? Did your sister stop bullying you when you joined the SAS? If not, I'm gonna definitely have to make friends with Spencer and see if he can persuade her to emigrate to Australia.

Good luck and have fun. GBTM soon.

Harry Riddles

From Dad **to** Harry
03 May 20:04 BST

My kid –

I'm so sorry about today. Your sister can be a little nasty, but I don't want you to start worrying just because she says all these horrible, scary things to you that are not going to happen. We're fine. Working at the SuperSave isn't the end of the world even if your sister says it is. In fact, I'm learning stuff your mum would be very, very interested in hearing. For example, did you know that at 7.15 every night, we have a half-price sale on everything that will be out of date the next day? This means our grocery bill will go down by HALF. And you know what else? It's kinda nice working with other people again. After 25 years in a room on my own, it's not so bad to have a change. Anyway I'm not going to be there long. So relax. Everything is going to be fine. I love ya and BTW – what's going on with *My Pet Zombie*?

Pups

From Harry **to** Dad
03 May 20:12 BST

I showed some models to Spencer when he came into the art room, but he laughed and said it was a really dumb idea for a movie.

From Dad **to** Harry
03 May 20:16 BST

What's he know? Horror is the hottest genre in Hollywood right now.

From Harry **to** Dad
03 May 20:21 BST

What's that mean?

From Dad **to** Harry
03 May 20:28 BST

It means horror movies are more profitable than all the others because everybody loves them and they are so cheap to make.

From Harry **to** Dad
03 May 20:30 BST

Not if you animate them.

From Dad **to** Harry
03 May 20:33 BST

If you really love *My Pet Zombie* and you believe
in it, then do it and don't worry what anybody else
says. The important thing is to get it made, because
most people don't.

Pups xxx

From Harry **to** Dad
03 May 20:51 BST

Do they do half price on chocolate deals at 7.15 at the SuperSave? If so, that could help... if I can't get the Dragons or Alison Hardman to give me money.

———————————————

From Dad **to** Harry
03 May 20:52 BST

Why would Alison Hardman invest in *MPZ*?

———————————————

From Harry **to** Dad
03 May 20:54 BST

Um. I'm just guessing that she wouldn't want to.

Would she?

From Dad **to** Harry
03 May 20:59 BST

NO! And you are much better off not having anything to do with that company. How many chocolate bars do you need? Maybe I'll invest in you.

From Harry **to** Dad
03 May 21:01 BST

35 bars a week. Maybe more.

From Dad **to** Harry
03 May 21:16 BST

Then you better do a budget and let me know the numbers.

From Harry **to** Dad
03 May 20:16 BST

What's a budget?

From Dad **to** Harry
03 May 20:12 BST

We'll do one tomorrow.

From Harry **to** Dad
03 May 20:14 BST

I love you, Pups.

_____

From Dad **to** Harry
03 May 20:15 BST

Love you too. Big time. xxx

CHAPTER TWELVE
AREA 51

Your dad is sk8boarding!
Walnut

What?
Harry

Ur dad is at Area 51! He can drop in!

B ryt there!!!

From Harry **to** Tony Hawk, Skateboard Legend
04 May 20:47 BST

Tony Hawk, King of All Sk8boarders, hi

My dad is like a really ANCIENT skater dude
who has not been on a skateboard for like 30
years, but has just decided he wants to start
sk8ing again. Good idea? Or plain dumb? I'm
worried, cos it's kinda my fault that he's skating
again. I found his old Alva pool board (the one
with the really cool reggae writing) out in our
barn and I showed it to him cos I thought it
might take his mind off all the stuff that's been
bothering him and he was like, "Wow – I forgot I
still had this baby." So then Walnut came round
with his board and started doing these power
slides around our kitchen floor and my dad was
watching and he said, "You're doing it wrong.

The Bertlemann slide is like this." And then my dad did one. And he was kind of psyched so he did another one. And then another. And then him and Walnut were like doing these slides all around the kitchen until my mum came in with some shopping and my dad crashed into her and before she got mad I said, "Don't get mad, Mum – it's my fault! I thought Dad might like to ride his board again." Amazingly, my mum thought it was a good idea.

Then my mum rented this movie for my dad called *Dogtown and Z Boys*. Have you seen it? My mum said my dad would love this film and he did! He said those guys were like his heroes when he was growing up and the next thing I know, my dad is down at Area 51 dropping in on the Wall of Death cos he's crazy.

My only worry is Walnut's dad. He got on a skateboard in a half-pipe like three months ago, fell off, knocked himself out and then had to go to hospital to have this big operation on his shoulder.

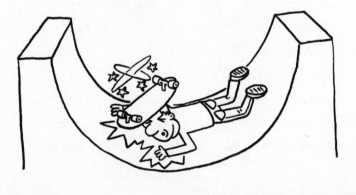

He still can't use it properly and it cost him like £5,000 to fix, so if my dad smashes anything it's gonna stay smashed cos we don't have £5,000, so that's something to think about, right? My sister says nobody over the age of 45 should skateboard. I told my sister Dad was a professional skateboarder when he was a kid and she said that was YEARS ago.

Do you still sk8? I saw that 900 you did at the X Games on YouTube and that was like the most awesome trick I've ever seen. Me and Walnut then looked at all the other videos and found the one of you riding that monster ramp at your friend's house and we thought, *Wow, you can still rip it on a ramp that's the size of a small mountain.* That's pretty incredible. And BTW – if my dad ever shows up at your friend's ramp? Don't let him ride it and don't listen to what he says, OK? He's not you. He will kill himself. His name is Wilson and he likes drinking beer and dancing with my mum. Thanks a lot.

Good luck and have fun.

Harry Riddles

BTW – your skateboard games totally RULE and if I could skate like I can play, I'd be better than you. HA!

Dad's not a fail. SuperSave is a really great job and he's not going to be doing it for long.
Harry

U r an idiot and a loser and v dumb. He's a fail and we're doomed.
Charlotte

Why do you think he's always walking around the house in the middle of the night? It's not cos he's having fun, moron.

He is when he's sk8ing. HA!

CHAPTER THIRTEEN
EVIL SISTER

This is a ransom note. Do _NOT_ tell <u>MUM</u> or <u>DAD</u>. I have kidnapped your cuddly monkey. Do as I say and the monkey will be returned to your bed at the end of Spencer's stay this weekend. You got that? My demands are:

1) Be nice to Spencer.
2) Treat him like the brother you wished I was.
3) Let him use your Xbox when he wants (but do not get into a marathon zombie shoot-out, or I will take the Xbox and you will never see it again).
4) Do not complain when Mum puts him in the spare bed in your room.
5) Don't eat all the pancakes on Sunday.

Do all of these things and I will return

your stupid monkey (without pulling off his arms or showing Jessica a picture of you and that stupid monkey). Remember – I am your EVIL SISTER, but stop leaving 'Come Visit Australia' brochures outside my bedroom. I HATE Australia.

Good luck and have fun, you little idiot. HA HA HA HA!

Charlotte

You should think of joining the Taliban. They could learn a lot from you. I hate you. If any harm comes to my monkey, I will take all your make-up and flush it down the toilet – got that u sicko?

HIS ROYAL HARRYNESS

Tresinkum Farm
Cornwall PL36 OBH
9th May

Harry Styles
Modest! Management
The Matrix Complex
91 Peterborough Rd
London SW6 3BU

Hi Harry –

Guess what? Remember that idiot I told you about? My sister's boyfriend, Spencer? Well, he's coming to stay at my house this weekend and I know you're probably way too busy to help me out, and you probably don't need any

more girlfriends, but I don't know who else
I can ask to help me get my monkey back. I
realise now you probably don't want to take
my sister with you on your world tour, but how
about if you called her up and told her that her
little brother has got her some free tickets to one
of your concerts and that if you gave him his
monkey back, you'd let her come backstage? I
know it's a lie, but I just want my monkey back
and I think maybe this is one of those times you
can tell a lie and get away with it.

Get back to me soon and let's rescue that
monkey before my sister rips his arms off.

Harry Riddles

BTW – do you ever get shy with girls? My sister
says you don't have to talk to girls, girls want
to talk to you because you're so famous. Is that

really how it works? What if you're not famous? What do you do then? I don't think I'm ever gonna get famous, so I don't know how I'm ever gonna get to talk to Jessica properly. Plus, Ed Bigstock has his eye on her and he's always putting me down in front of her. So what do you think I should do?

From Harry **to** Charley
Subject: My monkey
11 May 19:22 BST

Hey Cuz –

Are you lucky you don't have a psycho sister! Her new boyfriend came to stay at our house for the weekend and I thought I was going to throw up every time that kid went to bed. His feet STANK! Even with the window open. When I told him, he said the feet have more sweat glands than anywhere else in our bodies and it's not his fault he's a teenager and more prone to sweaty feet than anybody except pregnant women. I said he could try washing his feet before he went to bed. I'll bet pregnant women wash their feet. He said it didn't make any difference because he suffers from bromo-something, which means his feet always smell. So I said, "Why don't you just keep your shoes on for the weekend?" Which was fine until my sister found out and then she said I was being mean to him and not making him feel welcome and that my monkey was now on Death Row and unless there was a big improvement in my behaviour, my monkey was HISTORY. So you know what I did? Nose clips. But then my mum walked in to say goodnight and she saw the clips on my nose and she asked me what I was doing wearing nose clips in bed, so I told her it's either nose clips or my monkey gets executed.

Well, then it all came out and my mum got

really mad and told my sister not to kidnap my animals and to give me my monkey back and to stop being so horrible. So then they had this big argument and my sister said she was going to run away, but Spencer wasn't keen on running anywhere at 10 on a Saturday night in the pouring rain (he probably didn't have any petrol in his Micra), so he persuaded her to stay and she said, "I'll stay this time FOR SPENCER, but I'll be leaving AS SOON AS I CAN." So that was really good news and it got even better when I got my monkey back (with his arms still attached). The bad news is Spencer says *My Pet Zombie* really sucks, cos nobody wants to see cuddly zombies. So now I'm beginning to worry that if my zombies aren't scary, nobody will want to see my movie. What do you think?

Harry

From Charley **to** Harry
11 May 11:26 PDT

Zombies eat people, not carrots.

From Harry **to** Charley
11 May 19:29 BST

Well maybe they should start eating carrots and do something different.

From Charley **to** Harry
11 May 11:30 PDT

Think of something else.

From Harry **to** Steve Bakshall of the Deadly 60
11 May 20:04 BST

Steve Backshall, host of my favourite wildlife
show, hi there

I have a great idea for an animal to add to
your Deadly 60 list – my sister, Charlotte. I
know you like to track animals in their own
habitat but if you gave me a heads-up I could
tell my mum and dad you were coming round
and we could get out of your way while you
made your way up into the death zone, where
my sister spends most of her life on Facebook.
Plus, I could tell you why she should be put
on your list, her impact on the ecosystem of
my house (always fighting with my mum and
telling my dad he's a fail) and how she is such
a lethal predator (especially near my animals).

This could be a really great show, BTW. GBTM soon.

Harry Riddles

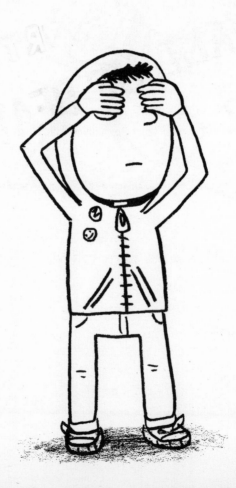

CHAPTER FOURTEEN
WALL OF DEATH

DRAFT EMAILS NOT YET SENT

From Harry **to** Jess

12 May 18:41 BST

Hi Jessica –

Are you busy this weekend? Would you like to come to the ballpark with me and Walnut? It's gonna be lots and lots of fun.

Harry

_____

12 May 18:44 BST

Hi Jess –

Guess what we're doing this weekend? Going to the beach to have a BBQ!!! You want to come?

Harry

12 May 18:49 BST

Hi Jessy –

D'you like dodgems? Or maybe you like the
Haunted House Ride?
I DON'T KNOW WHAT TO
WRITE!!!@@££@%$^&*

From Harry **to** Charley
13 May 16:14 BST

Cuz –

OMG you won't believe what happened on the school run this morning. Our car hates the rain and when it rains our car starts backfiring A LOT.

So we get to school – eventually – but the car is like going BANG! BANG! BANG! And when we finally pull up in the school car park at like 8.15, Jessica and her mum are sitting up on their horses (cos they sometimes ride to school across the moor), and I tell my dad, "You better turn the engine off quick," but before he does the car makes the most ENORMOUS bang, like a canon going off: BAAAAAANNNGGGGG!!!!!

Well, that was enough. Jessica's mum's horse reared up and then the animal bolted towards the rugby fields. Fortunately, Jessica's horse

didn't bolt, but we did nearly kill her mum, so I hid in the footwell and told my dad to go and say sorry and then I could sneak out the rear door and make a run for my classroom. But when I got out of the car, Jessica saw me and she called out and I thought, *OMG – what do I say to her?* So I went over and I said sorry and she said, "Thank you." I said, "What for?" And she said she'd been telling her mum for weeks that Thunderbolt was not ready to go anywhere, cos he was like super-frisky – and I just helped her prove her point and might even have saved her mum's life cos he did it at school and not on the open road. I don't think her mum saw it that way, but who cares? Me and Jessica were like talking and it wasn't about the school play. Then she asked me if I was a skater like Ed. I said, "I don't skate, but my dad does and he's like the oldest guy in the skate park but he really loves it, so what can you do?" She said my dad sounds like a cool guy and we laughed and I thought things were really going great, but then Bigstock turns up and tells her that I'm no skater like him. I'm just a stupid gamer. So I said I didn't know cleaning your teeth with the Wall of Death was a core skater skill and Jessica kind of laughed but before Ed could hit me, I took off. But maybe I should learn to sk8.

Harry

From Charley **to** Harry
13 May 08:16 PDT

You definitely should. It's fun.

From Harry **to** Charley
13 May 16:17 BST

I dunno about fun.

From Charley **to** Harry
13 May 08:19 PDT

You know what I think? You need to get out
more. In every way.

CHAPTER FIFTEEN
EAT THE PARENTS

From Dad **to** Harry
13 May 21:27 BST

My kid –

I'm really sorry about embarrassing you at
school. It was just one of those days when
I took my eye off the ball. And don't let
Charlotte wind you up about the fiscal cliff.
We're not going to be living in boxes. I'm
almost finished with this new thing and when
it's done, I'm going to send it off and then
everything will be back to normal again. OK?
BTW – what's going on with your film?

Pups

———————————

From Harry **to** Dad

14 May 21:29 BST

Pups –

That dipstick Spencer was right. Nobody wants to see cuddly zombies. Anyway, when I was at school today, some kids were talking about how strict their parents were and how much of a nightmare it was, trying to get online during school nights, and that's when I had a better idea. It's called *Eat the Parents* and I was thinking maybe you could help me make it over half term. What do you think?

From Dad **to** Harry
14 May 21:31 BST

I think I preferred *My Pet Zombie*.

From Harry **to** Dad
15 May 08:01 BST

Yeah, but *My Pet Zombie* sucks.

From Dad **to** Harry
15 May 13:12 BST

No, it doesn't.

From Harry **to** Dad
15 May 16:59 BST

It sucks.

From Dad **to** Harry
15 May 21:08 BST

Are you angry with us?

From Harry **to** Dad
15 May 21:11 BST

Sometimes, but not today.

From Dad **to** Harry
15 May 21:48 BST

Sure?

_____

From Harry **to** Dad
16 May 20:03 BST

Can't wait to move schools.

_____

From Dad **to** Harry
16 May 20:44 BST

You're not going to have to move schools.

_____

From Harry **to** Dad
16 May 20:47 BST

Promise?

From Dad **to** Harry
16 May 20:56 BST

When I sell this thing, we'll be fine. But how are you going to make an animated stop-motion if you don't have a stop-motion camera?

From Harry **to** Dad
17 May 16:32 BST

You are such a dinosaur, Pups – I got an app on my iPod. But the iPod doesn't have a stand so placing the iPod without it falling over is like really, really hard. So if you guys want to buy me a stop-motion camera with a tripod – they're like £70 online.

From Dad **to** Harry
17 May 20:49 BST

That's about what I make a day at SuperSave.

From Harry **to** Dad
17 May 20:49 BST

And that's why you need to HELP ME so you don't have to do that stupid job! And by the way, your manager is a real jerk. What's wrong with you talking to me? I'm your son.

From Dad **to** Harry
17 May 21:03 BST

What's your story?

From Harry **to** Dad
18 May 21:17 BST

Well, it's about a family kind of like ours. There's
this ten-year-old kid, his fifteen-year-old sister,
their mum and their dad, and they live in this
nice house with their dog, OK? Now the sister
is basically a psycho who is always angry and
always stealing stuff she shouldn't steal. Her
boyfriend is a gap-year musician who plays too
much Xbox and is probably a sex maniac. Those
are my main characters.

What happens is the sister and the boyfriend go off to the Zombies of Rock Festival and they get BITTEN by zombies. So when they come home, they are ZOMBIES. But Mum and Dad don't know their daughter is now a zombie. They just think she's tired and needs a hot bath and some good home cooking and then she'll be right as rain.

But the boy? He's not fooled. He KNOWS there's a reason his sister's backpack is swarming with FLIES – and it's not because she was rolling around in the mud at the Zombies of Rock Festival!!! It's because she's got an ARM or something in there.

So later that night, after everybody has gone to bed, the boy decides he has to go and investigate and find out what's in that backpack. So he creeps down the hall. He's terrified. But he knows HE'S the ONLY one who can save his family. So he gets to her door. He opens it S-L-O-W-L-Y and then he is BLINDED by white light. He screams. "AAAARGH!!!!!" You see where I'm coming from?

_____

From Dad **to** Harry
18 May 21:21 BST

Horror films often say more about the people
who make them and their fears than anything the
characters might say.

_____

From Harry **to** Dad
18 May 21:22 BST

It's just a zombie film, Dad.

_____

From Dad **to** Harry
18 May 21:24 BST

OK.

_____

From Harry **to** Dad
18 May 21:25 BST

Will you help me?

From Dad **to** Harry
18 May 21:27 BST

I'll try, but I'm really busy trying to finish my
thing, which is gonna be great.

From Harry **to** Dad
May 18 21:28 BST

Well, let's hope it's funny.

From Dad **to** Harry
18 May 22:48 BST

It's the best thing I've written.

CHAPTER SIXTEEN
REPORT CARD

From Dad **to** Harry
22 May 15:22 BST

Got this at work. We need 2 talk TONIGHT.

Dad

From: Malcolm Forbes
Date: 22 May 2014 10:39:36 BST
To: wilsonriddles@gmail.com
Subject: Assessment Card for HARRY
RIDDLES

Please find attached Harry's Half Term
Attainment & Effort Grades Sheet.

With kind regards,
Malcolm Forbes

Half Term Attainment & Effort Grades
Summer Term 2014
Riddles, Harry
Year 6 MF

	Attainment	Effort
English	B	3
Mathematics	C	2
Science	B	2
French	C	2
Latin	C	1
History	D	3
Geography	C	2
R.S	C	2
D.T	C	2
I.C.T	C	2
Art	A	4

Form Tutor's Comment:

Harry seems to be finding it very difficult to apply himself to his work this term and as a scholarship student these grades are very disappointing. Harry needs to work harder and stop drawing zombies or he will struggle in his coming exams. But I am pleased about his engagement with the school play. His technical ability to get the lighting-rig software up and running impressed all as it had defeated many who had tried before. So well done, Harry.

From Harry **to** Dad
Subject: My report card
22 May 16:48 BST

What's wrong with Cs? Unlike Ed Bigstock, I
didn't get any Fs. And at least I'm still GOING
to school. If you send me to Mount Doom, I'm
not sure I'll bother. Charlotte said I'm definitely
moving schools.

From Dad **to** Harry
22 May 16:48 BST

I don't want to hear you start talking like that, do
you understand? That is not good enough for you.

From Harry **to** Dad
22 May 16:51 BST

Why? You didn't get good enough grades. You didn't even finish school.

From Dad **to** Harry
22 May 16:53 BST

And that's why YOU should – or you'll end up like me.

From Harry **to** Dad
22 May 16:54 BST

What's wrong with you? I don't mind.

From Dad **to** Harry
22 May 16:59 BST

But I do – so start studying. And don't listen to
your sister. She doesn't know what's going on.
We're just waiting for some guys to read the script
and write a coverage report and when that comes
back, we're off to the races.

From Harry **to** Dad
22 May 17:01 BST

I hope so cos Charlotte says unless there's a
miracle the Riddles family are going over the
fiscal cliff and then who knows where we'll all
end up – maybe at the Reading Rock Festival in
a tent with her and Spencer, cos that's where
they're going to be on her sixteenth birthday.

From Dad **to** Harry
22 May 17:02 BST

Why is your sister going to Reading? We're going to Spain to see your grandparents!

From Harry **to** Dad
22 May 17:03 BST

Well, SHE'S not, even if WE are. And I think we'll have a MUCH better time without her. Think about it. You and me can go to the cable ski park and not spend the day getting bored on the beach while she tries to impress that skinny Spanish kid who rents the paddleboards by Victor's – which I'll bet she hasn't mentioned to Spencer, BTW.

From Dad **to** Harry
22 May 17:03 BST

And don't you mention it, either. Besides – what's wrong with coming on holiday with us?

From Harry **to** Dad
22 May 17:04 BST

She says Marbella is for losers. She wants to go to Ibiza. Or Reading. Or Glastonbury. Or anywhere we're not.

From Dad **to** Harry
22 May 17:04 BST

That's really sad.

From Mum **to** Harry
22 May 20:32 BST

Would you like me to take you to the longest zip wire in Cornwall when I get back from Grandma's this weekend? We haven't spent any time together for ages.

Mum

From Harry **to** Charley
24 May 21:12 BST

Hey Cuz –

I just went on the longest zip wire in Cornwall and it shoulda been really great, but my mum got

really upset when my dad called her in the car on the way home. He had some BAD news. The people who read his scripts in Hollywood and decide if they should buy them or not said they thought his script was 'basically humourless'.

That's what I heard my mum repeat on the phone and that made me think my sister is right. I'm definitely moving schools.

Harry

CHAPTER SEVENTEEN
FAMILY NIGHT

From Harry **to** Charley

25 May 20:48 BST

Hi Cuz –

You know when I told you some idiot wrote that my dad's last script was basically humourless and they shouldn't buy it? Well, he wasn't the only one. Three people have now said the same thing and I think my mum thinks it's time to inspire my dad to start thinking about doing something else for a career.

So my mum had this great idea how to get through to my dad without nagging him – by using the MOVIES. So she told us we were gonna have a FAMILY movie night and not watch *Britain's Got Talent* or *The Voice* or whatever – which we always have to watch with my sister, who wants to be a singer and thinks she could be as famous as One

Direction, if she could be bothered.

We had Spencer staying over and he was being a real suck-face trying to please my mum, pretending to be interested in her movies. So he's out in the kitchen telling Mum how he's like really 'intrigued' – he used that word (and I bet he doesn't even know what it means) – to see *Jerry Maguire* and *Out of Africa* (the two movies my mum had rented) and would encourage Charlotte to watch them too. So my mum said, "Spencer, what would I do without you? You're such a nice boy!"

Spencer started grinning at her in a way that made me think he's not half as nice as she thinks, so I'm gonna keep a close eye on that guy and if he starts washing his feet every ten minutes, I'll know what's going on.

Anyway we sit down in front of the TV and before my mum plays the DVD she gets up and makes this little speech to my dad saying here's two great stories about people who had crazy dreams, but they learned to sacrifice their DREAM for a BETTER dream: being HAPPY! I guess she was talking about this new career. Have you seen either of these two movies? Don't bother. Boring. We should have watched *Dunston*. Plus, when *Out of Africa* finished my mum was crying her eyes out cos this guy had crashed his plane and now had this lion sitting on his grave. My dad said if this is your mother's idea of how to be happy, we're in trouble. Predictably, Spencer said it was a great choice. That kid is such a lick-ass.

Harry

CHAPTER EIGHTEEN
SLAVES KICK BUTT

From Harry **to** Charley
26 May 16:16 BST

Hi Cuz –

Well, it's official. Me and Ed Bigstock are now definitely sworn enemies.

You remember I told you Ed said to Walnut that I was like his SLAVE at school? Well, we had this big Latin test and Mr Morton asks Ed to write on the whiteboard the Latin translation for MY SLAVE CARRIES SPEARS. Easy stuff. For normal kids. Not Ed. In fact, I doubt he could even spell that sentence in English. So Mr Morton goes to the bathroom and Ed's like panicking cos he's already on two strikes with Mr Morton, so he begs me to help him out and I think, *OK. Payback time*. So I slip him this piece of paper and he looks at it and he says, "Are you sure this is it, Harry?" And I'm like, "Yeah, Ed – that's what it is. Just write it up." So Mr Morton comes back in the room and Ed goes up to the whiteboard and he writes in big letters, SERVI KICKUS BUTTUS. Slaves kick butt. HA!

Well, when everybody had stopped laughing, Mr Morton gave Ed a detention for being the class clown and then gave me one too, cos Ed snitched on me. But you know what? It was worth it. Jessica came up to me after class and said what a shame it was that Ed was doing the school play, not me. Then we could practise our lines together, cos he's not taking the play very seriously and hasn't even LEARNED 'em! I told her acting's not really my thing, but you know what? Maybe it should be. She said, "Why don't I tell Mr Forbes you will be Ed's understudy because I know you know all the lines. You prompt Ed enough." So I say, "I don't think that's a good idea. I'm not really the acting type." Then she says, "How do you know you're not?" "Well," I say, "I like gaming." She says, "You should think about it, Harry." So I said I would. And I have. Acting sucks. But then I thought maybe I should take your advice and try and get out more. So I said to Jessica, "OK, I'll give it a try," and she said, "Great!" But then Ed found out and I don't think he liked having any competition, so he said to me, "You'll regret doing this, Harry. You mark my words, geek." What does THAT mean?

Harry

From Charley **to** Harry
26 May 08:17 PDT

Nothing. He's just trying to put you off your game. Ignore him.

From Harry **to** Charley
26 May 16:18 BST

I tried, but then he started laughing at me and I said something really stupid.

From Charley **to** Harry
26 May 08:18 PDT

What?

From Harry **to** Charley
26 May 16:19 BST

I said I was going to get Sam Mendes to come to the school play to watch Jessica, which is something Ed could NEVER do.

From Charley **to** Harry
26 May 08:19 PDT

Well, that was dumb.

From Harry **to** Charley
26 May 16:29 BST

I know, but I had to say something and when I said it, Oscar Da Silva said, "Of course Harry can get Sam Mendes to come to the play – he's a friend of your dad's, right?" And before I can answer, Jessica says, "I knew your dad was cool!" And then Ed says, "Your dad knows Sam Mendes?" And I see him glaring at me, like he's challenging me. So now I've got my back to the wall and before I can stop myself, I said, "Of course he does. My dad works in Hollywood. That's what he does. Sam Mendes is like a family friend." So Jessica asks me if I know Kate Winslet and I don't know who she is so I didn't lie, I said, "Not really."

Well, that did it. Now everybody in my school

thinks my dad and Sam Mendes are best friends and Sam Mendes is coming to the school play and my family are really hooked up with all these famous people. It's a nightmare. Even the teachers are looking at me different. I just hope term ends before Ed Bigstock turns up at the SuperSave and I become the school joke. What do you think I should I do?

From Charley **to** Harry
26 May 20:02 PDT

Write to him.

CHAPTER NINETEEN
SAM MENDES

From Harry **to** Sam Mendes

27 May 20:16 BST

Dear Sam Mendes –

Please, please, please can you help me, cos I'm
in lots of trouble. Everybody in my school now
thinks you are coming to see our school play, but
I haven't heard back from you and I don't know
what to do cos it's kind of got out of control.

All the mums who've got kids in the play are now
ringing up Mr Forbes and asking him if their kids
can get given bigger parts cos they all think you're

gonna be there and you might want to put their kid in your next movie. But you're not. Or are you? If you want, you could stay at our house. Will you think about it? I can teach you World of Zombies if you don't know how to play it.

Sorry.

Harry

From Dad **to** Harry
28 May 13:22 BST

Any idea what this is about?

From Malcolm Forbes, Deputy Head of
Pastoral Care **to** Wilson Riddles

Hi Wilson –

We haven't seen much of you at school this
term. Next time you come in – could we have
a little chat? Nothing too urgent. You know
where I am.

Best,
Malcolm

From Harry **to** Dad
28 May 16:42 BST

Probably wants to know if you want me to act in the school play.

_____

From Dad **to** Harry
28 May 16:58 BST

Why would he want to do that?

_____

From Harry **to** Dad
28 May 16:59 BST

All the parents want their kids in the play cos they think Sam Mendes is coming.

_____

From Dad **to** Harry
28 May 17:03 BST

Sam Mendes is coming to the school play?

_____

From Harry **to** Dad
28 May 17:30 BST

Maybe.

_____

From Dad **to** Harry
28 May 17:45 BST

That's great! How did you manage that?

_____

From Harry **to** Dad
28 May 17:46 BST

It's a long story.

Mum to Harry

Is Sam Mendes really coming
to see your school play?
Mum

Maybe.
Harry

From Harry **to** Charley
29 May 16:32 BST

Hey Cuz –

My dad told me this morning that he's going
to talk to Sam Mendes at the school play and if
they click, he's going to give him a script and this
could jump-start his career again. I tried to tell
my dad Sam probably wasn't going to come cos
he's thinking about doing another movie, but my
dad was in such a great mood, I didn't have the
guts to tell him the truth, but when he doesn't
turn up, everybody's gonna get really mad with
me. So maybe it's a good job I'm moving schools.
What do you think?

———————————————

From Charley **to** Harry
28 May 19:53 PDT

Get somebody else.

HIS ROYAL HARRINESS

Tresinkum Farm
Cornwall PL36 OBH
UK
31st May

Michael Bay
c/o Bay Films
2110 Broadway
Santa Monica, CA 90404
USA

Michael Bay, Director of *Transformers*, hi

My name is Harry Riddles and I just wanted
to say *Transformers* is my second-favourite
movie of all time behind *Dunston* (no offence).

If I was allowed we'd watch *Transformers*
every Saturday night because *Dunston* isn't
a movie I can watch more than once a year
without getting into a fight with my sister,
but she thinks the kid in *Transformers* is really
cool, so we can watch that a lot more.

The reason I'm writing is there's this girl
in my class called Jessica and I wanted to do
something really great for her before I have
to move schools, so I kinda told her that
this movie director was gonna come to our

school play to watch her act and she got really
excited, but I don't think he's gonna show, so
that's why I'm writing to you.

Would you like to come to our school play?
I don't know if Jessica is good or whatnot,
but I like her and I thought all you can do is
say no to me and then at least I know I tried.
Plus, maybe you could talk to Mr Forbes
and get him to wrap his star in cotton wool,
because I really don't want to have to make
my stage debut if the star breaks his neck or
something doing parkour.

BTW – I hope you do at least twenty more *Transformer* movies and if you do, could you put some zombies in them? My dad said that's pretty unlikely, but I'm keeping my fingers crossed. So good luck with that, and I hope you're having fun, cos I'm definitely not.

Harry Riddles

CHAPTER TWENTY
SHOT LIST

World of ZOMBIES Community Forum

 Kid Zombie: Whassssup?

 Goofykinggrommet: Nothing.
Whassup with you?

 Kid Zombie: I don't know.

 Goofykinggrommet: Did you make
your movie?

Kid Zombie: Which one?

 Goofykinggrommet: Either.

 Kid Zombie: Not yet. I'm waiting for my dad but I don't know if he's going to help.

 Goofykinggrommet: Why not?

 Kid Zombie: Cos he's like working on this thing he wants to give to this movie guy.

 Goofykinggrommet: Who? Daniel Craig?

 Kid Zombie: Sam Mendes.

Goofykinggrommet: Is he coming?

 Kid Zombie: No.

 Goofykinggrommet: Have you told your dad?

 Kid Zombie: I tried but he didn't listen and now it's too late.

 Goofykinggrommet: Why?

 Kid Zombie: Cos ever since he found out this guy was coming he's been like Mr Great Dad. Even my mum noticed he's been in this great mood – even when he's working a double. He comes home, makes coffee, then goes out to his office and doesn't come back till late cos he's trying to finish something to show to this guy. And he told my mum, if this doesn't work, he'll definitely get a job as a teacher.

 Goofykinggrommet: You gotta tell him.

 Kid Zombie: Why? It's the first time he's been happy in months.

From Dad **to** Harry
04 June 02:07 BST

My li'l Mogulman –

If you want to make *Eat the Parents*, what you're going to need is a shot list. So I did this for you. I hope it helps.

Eat the Parents shot list:
  1) If your story starts at the Zombies of Rock Festival – maybe what you should do is have your sister and Spencer arrive at the festival site in daylight. (What's your set look like? A barbed-wire fortress? Or maybe just a big gate with some zombie security goons? Make it simple – you don't need a big set, just some steel doors with graffiti on them.) So they

arrive, bang on the doors and the zombie security guards let them inside. That's your first shot: S and C enter the zombie fest.

2) Then you stay on the door and you make the set go dark, so we know it's now NIGHT and on your soundtrack we hear the ROCK CONCERT and also the SCREAMING and the DEVOURING and the RIPPING OF HUMAN FLESH as the zombies start eating each other. The trick here is to get the audio track right, but I can help you mix that on my laptop.

3) Then daylight comes. And your sister and Spencer exit. And they have bloody mouths. And they are looking a little weary after a night of eating, devouring and

raving. And maybe they are snacking on
some tasty body parts?

4) Next you need them arriving back here and
being met by us. There's no way you'll
have the time to make a model of our place,
but you could blow up a photo in iPhoto
and lay that against a box or something.

5) Next you're going to need some close-ups.
You'll need Dad saying, "Welcome home!"
And then your mum saying, "You guys
look really tired – did you have fun?" And
then Spencer moaning or grunting like a
dumb zombie and maybe a human finger
falls out of his pocket? Or he spits out a
human nail?

6) Anyway, Spencer and your sister go inside

the house and your mum says, "They're just tired!" But you're not convinced.

7) Now you'll probably need a time transition shot of the house going from day to night, so we'll know it's dinner time for the Riddles family.

8) Now you need to do the interiors. So why don't you start with everybody sitting at the kitchen table about to have dinner?

9) Next you need a close-up of a steaming fish pie as it's brought to the table and put down.

10) Now a close-up of your mum saying, "I made a fish pie – your favourite, Charlotte!"

Now a shot of Charlotte, grunting, because Charlotte has had a change in dietary needs after her transformation into a flesh-eating zombie. A tasty fish pie doesn't quite do it for her any more. She wants fresh meat – US!

11) So now we see Spencer and Charlotte decline the fish pie. Your mum says, "But you've got to eat something!" And your sister says ominously, "We're gonna eat later." Then they get up and leave the table.

12) Now YOU try and warn us that we're in BIG trouble, but we won't listen because we're having a glass of wine and listening to some French dudes play disco.

13) So now we need to go back outside the house and in this shot we see the farm again just before bedtime. All the lights inside are on. We hear your mum say, "Bedtime!" Now all the lights go out and the whole house is dark.

14) Next we need a shot of a full moon, maybe with the clouds moving across it – which lets your audience know: TROUBLE IS ON THE WAY!

15) So now we go into your bedroom and we see you up in your bed with your million cuddly toys, lying there in the moonlight. You can't sleep. You're worried you have some zombies in your house and nobody but YOU knows this. So you get up. You walk over to the door. You open the door

slowly and… AAAAARGH!!!! Mum and
Dad are waiting for you!!! And they're
flesh-eating ZOMBIES!!! URRRRRR!!!

Something like that? Is that really what you want
to do? It's a bit dark, isn't it?

Pups xxxx

Spencer to Harry

I saw your dad's shot list and I love *Eat The Parents*. I want to write some music for you!
Spencer

I don't have any money. Or chocolate.
Harry

For free. I love *Eat The Parents*!!

From Harry **to** Dad
05 June 11:31 BST

No, it's not dark. It's gonna be GREAT!!! Even Spencer likes it – and he's eighteen!

CHAPTER TWENTY-ONE

DINGBAT

From Harry **to** Charley
8 June 19:48 BST

Hey Cuz –

You won't believe what happened here this weekend. My mum told my dad she had to go up to London to talk to the Germans and make sure they liked her new work.

So basically she leaves us with some pizzas, but before she goes she tells my dad what a great opportunity this will be for the two of us to bond and hang out together. And I'm thinking, *Oh really? I don't think so*. So she goes and my dad says, "Look, I know your mum thinks you and me are going to have this great bonding experience, but I have to get my work finished cos this is the only way things can ever get better for us, so you'll have to make that movie on your own, all right?"

So now I'm thinking, *OK, what about* my *movie? Who says my movie isn't going to change things round here? I gotta make it but the one guy I really need to help me is not going to help me cos he's working on a project for some guy he'll never meet and will never give him a job, cos he's not coming! So what do I do? Tell him? What if he gets depressed? That's not going to help.* So I thought, *I know, I should let him finish his thing. THEN I'll tell him.*

So I didn't say a word and thank god it rained non-stop in Cornwall and there was like no surf, cos my friend Walnut had nothing better to do but hang out at my house. So he came over and basically we made the movie in my kitchen,

which was like really cool – except for the last bit
when we had a total DISASTER and everything
was RUINED.

Basically what happened was we had this one
final thing we had to film where the kid discovers
his parents have been turned into flesh-eating
ZOMBIES. So we set everything up. We made
these really cool zombie models of my mum
and my dad. We stuck them in our set that we
made of our house. Then we set the camera up
and turned the kitchen lights on and off, so it's
like this big, scary thunderstorm kind of deal.
And then we get the little kid creeping down the
dark corridor in the middle of this terrible storm.
And we get all these cool close-ups of him acting
really, really scared. And we get all the way to the
part with him opening the door and you know
what happens next? Stupid Dingbat STEALS my

parents and EATS THEM! I think he thought they were like rabbits or something! And I'd just told my dad, "DO NOT LET THE DOG IN THE HOUSE!" But he lets Dingbat in the house when he comes in to make some coffee and Dingbat's head DIVES into our shot and STEALS our models and DESTROYS our set! And basically that's it! We've run out of time! So now we have this stupid film

– which was great until Dingbat RUINED it. That dog needs glasses and a muzzle. But I'll upload it anyway and see what happens. Knowing our luck, not much – unless dogs like watching YouTube.

Harry

From Charley **to** Harry
8 June 20:31 PDT

Watched your movie, man. HILARIOUS. I'm posting it on my Facebook page. Nice work, smurf.

CHAPTER TWENTY-TWO
TROUBLE

From Charley **to** Harry
15 June 02:49 PDT

Hey – you know how many likes I got for your film? 28 and counting!

From Harry **to** Charley
15 June 10:51 BST

What are you doing up? Isn't it like 3am?

From Charley **to** Harry
15 June 02:53 PDT

World of Zombies, man. U wanna play?

From Harry **to** Charley
15 June 10:53 BST

I got other stuff to worry about.

From Charley **to** Harry
15 June 02:54 PDT

Like what?

From Harry **to** Charley
15 June 10:54 BST

Like I may just have done something really dumb.

From Charley **to** Harry
15 June 02:55 PDT

What's new?

From Harry **to** Charley
15 June 10:56 BST

No, really. This is seriously very dumb and could
get me in a LOT of TROUBLE.

From Charley **to** Harry
15 June 02:59 PDT

What have you done?

_____

From Harry **to** Charley
15 June 11:00 BST

I mighta written to somebody I shouldn't have
written to.

_____

From Charley **to** Harry
15 June 03:01 PDT

Who? Jessica?

_____

From Harry **to** Charley
15 June 11:01 BST

My teacher.

From Charley **to** Harry
15 June 03:02 PDT

Saying what?

From Harry **to** Charley
15 June 11:02 BST

I'll tell you ONLY if you keep it on the QT.

From Charley **to** Harry
15 June 03:03 PDT

Tell.

_____

From Harry **to** Charley
15 June 11:06 BST

OK. So, fifteen minutes ago I'm out in my dad's office and I'm building this cool new monster on Spore and *ping*! My dad gets an email notification. I see it's from Mr Forbes at my school. *Uh-oh!* I think. I know exactly what this is about – Ed Bigstock and my Latin detention. Do I open the mail? I'm not meant to, but I'm really curious. So I open the mail and I find out Mr Forbes wants an urgent meeting to discuss... ME!!!

Well, if Mr Forbes tells my mum and my dad that he thinks I've become a TROUBLEMAKER on top of my poor grades, they'll definitely take away my dad's laptop and then HOW am I gonna make this family some money to come visit you guys? Not going to happen, right?

So, I think, *Maybe if I write back to Mr Forbes and pretend to be my dad, I can put him off.* I know I shouldn't, but I think, *What the hell, I'm probably not going to be at this school next term, what does it matter?* Right?

So I write, *Hi Malcolm, I'm out in China making a movie and I will not be returning to the UK until July 20th. OK? Sorry. Thanks.* Then I press send and now I'm feeling scared, cos this is not stuff I normally do and if my parents find out I'm gonna

be grounded for like YEARS. Worse, I realise Mr Forbes is DEFINITELY gonna want to write back. And when he does, my dad will see the mail, then he'll find out what I just did and then I'll be toast. So I think, *OK, maybe I better write ONE last mail and stop him.* So I write another one, saying, *Oh, by the way, I will not be able to pick up any of my emails until AFTER July 10th so please, please, please do NOT try and get in touch with me. OK? And do not contact my wife because her email is broken cos she hasn't paid her bill.* So I send that and now I'm feeling really, really anxious and may be about to have a panic attack cos I started yawning a LOT and my stomach was churning. But there's like no way they're not going to find out, right? What do you think? Should I tell my dad? I'm not good at keeping this stuff secret.

Harry

From Charley **to** Harry
15 June 03:09 PDT

He'll find out anyway.

From Harry **to** Charley
15 June 11:10 BST

How?

From Charley **to** Harry

15 June 03:11 PDT

If he's got a smartphone, he'll get mail on it,
you idiot.

From Harry **to** Charley

17 June 20:24 BST

OK, so guess what happened with the phone
thing? After you mailed me (and how come your
dad doesn't BUST you for staying up so late?) I
remembered my dad is not allowed to carry his
phone whilst he's working – which means he can
only check his phone during lunch break. Which
means I had like 49 minutes to get down to
SuperSave and stop him reading his mail. Or I'd
spend the next ten years in my room doing Time

Out. So I tell my mum, "I have to go see Dad, can you give me a ride so I can get a bus? But like now? Please? Emergency?"

So my mum takes me down to the village and I jump on the first bus, thinking, *Yay I'll have plenty of time to get to town.* But then the bus breaks down on the Atlantic Highway and I've only got like twenty minutes to get there, so I start running like a maniac and who should stop? Jessica and her mum! They are on the way to buy a new wetsuit for Jessica. So they offer me a lift and as soon as I get in the car, Jessica's mum tells me how excited she is that Sam Mendes is coming to the school play! What a great incentive for all the kids to raise their game!

"Yeah," I say. "It is pretty amazing, isn't it? What a nice guy." And Jessica's mum says, "Maybe he'll bring Daniel Craig too!" I said, "I doubt it, but you never know, right?" And she says she LOVES Daniel Craig. I tell her all mums do. And then she starts asking me how I knew Sam Mendes – was he a good friend of my dad's? And Jessica said, "Yes, because Harry's dad writes for the MOVIES."

So then her mum starts asking me what movies my dad has done, and would she have seen any of them, and how much she loves the movies and would love to talk to my dad about them! So that was like pretty awkward and I tried not to lie any more but the damage was done and basically, it's only a matter of time before this whole thing comes crashing down on my head and buries me for ever and ruins any chance I might have of going out with Jessica. So I can't wait to get out that car but before I go Jessica's mum says maybe we should all have a BBQ on the beach when term ends. And if Sam Mendes is staying, he could come too! "Sure, I'll find out," I say.

Before I can get out of the car, Jessica writes their number on some paper and asks me if I want to come to her birthday party. I say. "I'd like that very much. Thank you."

So they drop me off and I run into the SuperSave and I'm five minutes early and I think, *At least I got here before my dad's break,* but when I get inside, my dad's manager tells me my dad took an early lunch. So I think, *That's it. I'm cooked.* But then I find my dad in the coffee shop and he's looking at his phone and he has forgotten his glasses so he can't read his mail so he asks ME to read the emails to him. I take the phone and

I see he's got like six new mails and one of them is the one from Mr Forbes. "Which ones do you want me to read?" I ask. "All of 'em," he says.

So I read every single one except the one from Mr Forbes. He says, "Wasn't there one from Mr Forbes?" And I'm thinking, *You know what? I'm not going to lie any more. I'm gonna tell the truth and take the punishment and if I get banned from World of Zombies, then I get banned from World of Zombies and five elite gaming prestiges* (I got two more last week) *is not a bad way to go.* So I open the mail and it says: *Good luck with your film. See you soon. Malcolm.* And I think, *What?* So I read it to my dad, and my dad thinks Mr Forbes is talking about something completely different, so he says, "How did he know I was writing a new movie? Did you tell him I was writing something?" "Um. Maybe," I say. "What a nice man," says my dad. "You're such a lucky kid going to that school." Let's hope I stay there, I say. I was too shocked to say anything else, so for now it looks like I got away with it.

From Charley **to** Harry
17 June 17:16 PDT

I doubt it.

_____

From Harry **to** Charley
18 June 08:01 BST

Thanks.

_____

From Charley **to** Harry
18 June 07:58 PDT

Seriously – it's only a matter of time before he NAILS you. And what's the deal with Jessica? You going to her party?

_____

From Harry **to** Charley
18 June 16:34 BST

I don't know. Maybe. But I got to figure out what
I can get her.

Send us an email

*Title: Mr / Mrs / Miss: Mr

*Last name: Riddles

*First name: Harry

*Email: harryriddles1@gmail.com

Address: Tresinkum Farm

*City/State/Territory: Cornwall

*Country: UK

Phone Number:

Please select the subject of your enquiry:
General enquiry

Are you already a Harry Winston Client?
Yes / No: No

Dear Harry Winston, jeweller to the STARS

My dad said you guys supply all the best jewels to all the biggest movie stars at the Oscars. Well, it's my friend Jessica's eleventh birthday in a couple of weeks and I was wondering if you guys could lend us some stuff to make her feel good when the big day comes.

My mum says you gave Charlize Theron some vintage bracelets worth over four million dollars and they had over a hundred carats in them (which I think you've misspelt by the way). I don't know where you get your carrots from but I think you're being ripped off. Farmer Harold could sell you a hundred nice Cornish carrots for less than five pounds, but I know yours will look a lot nicer round Jessica's neck then Farmer Harold's.

If publicity is what you're after, I know Jessica's mum will have her daughter's birthday pictures in *The Dartmoor Dart*, which has got like TONS of readers. And don't worry about security, cos nobody can get in our house without getting past Dingbat. And he's a scary dog if you wake him up in the middle of the night.

Please help me make her day a birthday she'll never forget.

Good luck and have fun.

Harry Riddles

From Harry **to** Harry Winston
28 June 11:03 BST

Dear Harry Winston,

Thank you for sending me your Ultimate Bridal Collection, which BTW looks really great but might be jumping the gun a bit. We haven't even started dating so perhaps you could send it to me again in like twenty years? Thank you.

Harry Riddles

CHAPTER TWENTY-THREE
DEAR DEIDRE

From Harry **to** Dear Deidre, Agony Aunt, the *Sun*
01 July 20:06 BST

Dear Deirdre –

I wonder if you could help me. I don't want to
tell you my full name cos my dad reads your
newspaper every day and he's got enough on his
plate right now. But I am ten years old and I live
in Cornwall, so why don't you call me X.

There's a girl in my class I really like but I'm
scared of telling her how much I like her in case
she laughs at me. Plus, I think she likes this other
kid who is kind of an idiot. I can't tell you his
name, but he sucks at Latin.

Anyway, yesterday Year 6 had an art trip to
Delamore Gardens and the girls went on one

bus and the boys went on another and when we get to Delamore, my friend George Tibbs, who is crazy about this girl called Milly, gets off the bus and runs up to Milly and tells her how much he really, really missed her. The bus ride was only forty-five minutes so it was not really a big deal, but it was for him, because he just wanted to be with HER.

And that's kind of how I feel about this girl. It's nearly the summer holidays and I want to say to her how much I REALLY like her and want to hang out with her, but I can't. What do I do?

X

From Dear Deidre, Agony Aunt, the *Sun* **to** Harry
02 July 10:52 BST

Hi Harry, thanks for your email. I am sorry you are
so worried at the moment. I'm pleased you felt you
could write to me and I hope I'll be able to help you.

You tell me that you're ten and you really like a girl in
your class but you don't know how you can tell her.
Harry, the feelings you have are normal and natural
and if you want to tell her how you feel, that is up to
you. She may feel very flattered that you like her. I
am sending you my leaflet called 'Learning to Love',
which explains what we go through when we first
find somebody we like. I do hope it helps you. My
leaflet on shyness is also attached, which may help
you to feel more confident about yourself.

By the way, I never use names in my column so I felt

it was OK to call you by your name as my email is just to you. Thanks for writing and I do hope you can work things out.

All the best

Deidre

From Harry **to** Deidre
03 July 20:22 BST

Dear Deidre –

Thanks for writing back to me and sending me those great leaflets. The OVERCOMING SHYNESS one was definitely more interesting for me than the LEARNING TO LOVE one, but they were both great, so thanks a lot.

You know in the leaflet you said *your tongue is like lead and you stand there in stupid silence?* Well that's me when I try talking to Jessica. Last weekend her mum invited me to her birthday party, which I didn't know if I wanted to go to because Harry Winston didn't want to lend me any diamonds with carrots in them, but I did go and now I kinda wish I hadn't. But that's not your fault. It's Ed Bigstock's.

Good luck and have fun.

Harry Riddles

From Harry **to** Charley
06 July 19:14 BST

Hey Cuz –

I went to Jessica's party at the w/e. What a
disaster. Basically what happened was my dad
dropped me at her house and it was like a really
nice warm day, so we had this BBQ out in the
garden and then we went kayaking on the river
and then we went back to her house for tea and
cake and just before the parents came to pick us
up, we played Twenty-one Dares.

Have you ever played Twenty-one Dares? It's like
the BEST game if you want to date somebody
in your class, but you're too scared to ask.
What you do is you LOSE the game, and then
everybody DARES you to ask somebody out on

a date. That's kind of how it works. So I lost the game and I'm thinking, *Great, here's my big chance. They'll make me ask Jessica on a date.* But Ed Bigstock comes over and he's still pretty mad at me because of what happened in Latin, so he goes, "Why don't you tell Jessica who's NOT coming to the school play, Harry? I dare you!!! I have some bad news, everybody!"

Well, I was pretty sure Ed had somehow found out that my dad worked in SuperSave, not in Hollywood, so the game was now up and it was just a matter of time before everybody knew that I'd made it all up. So what do I do?

Well, I didn't have to do anything cos Ed was so excited he was about to pee his pants. So he points at me and said, "You lied, Harry!" And I think, *OK.* And Ed said, "Sam Mendes is NOT

coming to see our play because he has decided
to direct the next BOND movie!" And I thought,
Is that all you got? Yay! Result!

Jessica said, "Is that true?" I said, "I don't know.
Is he?" Ed said, "He is – and how come you didn't
know if he's such a good family friend?" Then
Ed pushed me into a wall and said, "Stop LYING,
Harry!" But Jessica told him to leave me alone

cos she doesn't think I'd lie because I'm nice,
which made me feel even worse. So now I better
get somebody famous to come to our school play
or Jessica will never believe anything I ever say
ever again. What do I do?

From Charley **to** Harry
06 July 11:21 PDT

Lol.

From Harry **to** Charley
06 July 19:23 BST

You're a big help.

CHAPTER TWENTY-FOUR
MORE TROUBLE

From Harry **to** Charley
08 July 20:21 BST

Hi Cuz –

OK, you know I might have said I was in big
trouble before with the Sam Mendes problem?
That's small change compared to what just
happened. I was sitting in the coffee shop at the
SuperSave doing my homework with my dad,
when Mr Forbes walks in for the first time ever.
Why he's shopping at SuperSave, I have no idea,
cos he lives right on the other side of the moor
in the middle of nowhere, so I'm thinking, *Oh my
god – why r u here?*

I try and hide behind my laptop, but Mr Forbes
spots my dad standing behind the counter

wearing his uniform. Mr Forbes does a double take cos clearly he's not expecting to see my dad working at the local supermarket. But there he is. Serving coffee. So Mr Forbes goes over to my dad and says, "Wilson, I thought you were out in China working on a film?" And my dad says he wishes he was out in China working on a film, but unfortunately he's here working at the SuperSave. Why?

Well then Mr Forbes sees me sitting in the booth. "Do you know anything about this, Harry?" he asks. "Maybe," I say, because I'm trying not to lie any more. Mr Forbes then tells my dad that he wanted my dad to come in and have a chat about me, but he got this email saying that my dad couldn't come to the school because he was out in China working on a film. Then he said he presumed my dad did NOT write that email?

"Clearly not," my dad says. "Well, I wonder who could have written it?" said Mr Forbes, looking right at me.

So now my face is like GLOWING and my dad says, "You've got some explaining to do, Harry." Mr Forbes says, "Why don't you two sort this out between you? And then come in and see me at school and we can have a meeting?" *Great. Look forward to it, I don't think.*

So Mr Forbes goes and my dad says, "Who else have you been writing to, Harry?"

So I tell him and he thinks about it. Then he says how pleased he is that I've started writing because writing's a good thing to do and a lot better than spending all my time playing World of Zombies. I say, "Thanks, Dad." And now I'm thinking this is going a LOT better than I had expected. But then he says writing as him is wrong. Why did I do it?

So I tell him about Ed and the Latin test and my detention and my movie and how I know it was wrong, but if I'm not going back to my school next year, what does it matter? Really? I mean, at Mount Doom they'd probably give me a commendation for WRITING an email to a teacher.

Well then I don't know what happened. My dad got angry and said I should stop being such a shoutykid because everything was going to be fine, but I told my dad everything wasn't going to be fine. Moving schools is not FINE and having to live in BOXES is not fine and him giving up his dream is not FINE – not for ME. And it shouldn't be for HIM, either.

Well, my dad didn't know what to say to that. He like stood there, blinking at me, like he was in shock. So then I told him Sam Mendes wasn't coming either. So all this work he's been doing in his office? No point.

My dad just looked at me like he didn't know what to think. So I left and I guess my dad musta been really upset cos that night instead of coming home after work he went down to the pub. And when he left the pub, he got in trouble with the police and now he has to go to court and my mum says he might lose his driving license and if that happens then she'll have to do all the driving everywhere and that's going to make our life really HARD.

And that's my fault.

Harry

From Charley **to** Harry
08 July 21:34 PDT

Hey – we all make mistakes. You're just a kid. Don't beat yourself up about it. It's not your fault. Your dad made the wrong choice. And BTW – *Eat the Parents* has got 52 likes.

Charley

From Harry **to** Simon Crow & Company Solicitors
09 July 20:52 BST

Hi Simon –

My mum said you need letters about my dad to
show to the judge what a good guy my dad is.
Well, I found a website that shows you what to
write, so here's mine.

Harry

Bodmin (East Cornwall) Magistrates' Court
Launceston Road, Bodmin, Cornwall
England, PL31 2AL
9th July
Court number 1289

To the Presiding Magistrate,

My name is Harry Riddles and I have known the accused, Winston Riddles, all my life since he is my DAD. My dad is a really good dad who is community-minded and has spent the last two and a half months helping the kids at my local skate park build a killer set of ramps, which has been great for the kids, but not so good for my mum, who wishes he spent more time at home doing stuff around the house, like changing light bulbs and mowing the lawn and taking the bin bags out when they're full.

That's not to say my dad's not family-minded. My dad is really family-minded. When he's not working at SuperSave, or building skate ramps for the community, he's helping me with my homework or helping me make my movie, or if he's not doing that he's picking my sister up from Spencer's house at like one in the morning, which he did last Saturday, because she and Spencer had this big argument about one of Spencer's old girlfriends who keeps texting him – and not many dads would do that, right? Even if my sister is a living nightmare. But my dad did. He drove all the way down to Dartmoor from my house, which is like miles and miles, just to pick up my sister cos she was really upset, and that's the kind of dad my dad is.

And whenever my mum needs help carrying shopping in from the car? My dad comes out of his office to help. She might have to shout at him, but he'll do it and I know for a fact Ed Bigstock's dad wouldn't do that – but then that guy spends most of his life walking to the North Pole or wherever, so he's not around much.

Ed's dad

my dad

Does my dad feel remorse for what happened?
He definitely does. My dad said what he did
was stupid and he can't believe he showed such
terrible judgement, but he was upset and not
thinking straight and that's why he went down
to the pub, which is not what he usually does
after work because what he usually does is
come home to work on his stuff, but he didn't
that night.

Why was he upset? Lots of reasons. Working at
the SuperSave sucks. His supervisor is an idiot.
His last movie *Bad Monkey* didn't do great, but
you can still find it in the DVD bin at SuperSave
and it only costs 50p (which is really good value
if you want to watch a great comedy) and it will
be a download soon. Also, the Getz Agency said
his last script was basically humourless, which
sucks if you write funny films. Which is why my

mum told him she thinks it's time he thought about taking a teaching job. But the really big thing that upset him was ME. I got in trouble at school with Mr Forbes and now Mr Forbes wants to speak with my parents and my dad thinks it's all his fault that I'm not doing so good at school and it's all his fault that I'm unhappy and that's basically why he went to the pub. I hope this helps him because my dad's the best dad in the whole world.

Harry Riddles

From Simon Crow to Harry
10 July 21:34 BST

Dear Harry –

Thank you very much for your letter. I think it will
be most helpful.

Best wishes,
Simon Crow

CHAPTER TWENTY-FIVE

BETTER THAN SAM MENDES

From Dad **to** Harry

12 July 20:47 BST

Little Big Man –

I'm so sorry about getting angry with you the other
night. And you know what? You're right. This is
not good enough for us but I needed to hear it from
somebody and you told me, so thank you. I don't
know what I'm going to do yet, but I will think of
something and when I do, I'll tell you what's going
on, OK?

In the meantime, I've asked my friend Tom
Witherspoon to come and see your school play.
Remember Tom? TV director buddy? We made
a few things together? He wants to find a place
to get married in Cornwall, so I told him he
could come and stay with us AS LONG AS HE

AGREED to come see *The Scarlet Pumpernickel* and he said, fine, he'd like that very much – so now you can tell Jessica that you haven't let her down, and that a successful TV director is coming to see her. Does that help you out?

Pups xxxxx

From Harry **to** Dad
12 July 20:51 BST

He's not Sam Mendes.

From Dad **to** Harry
12 July 20:55 BST

He's won more Emmys than Sam Mendes. And he's

won a Brown Bear at the Berlin Film Festival. And he makes family entertainment. What more do you want?

From Harry **to** Dad
12 July 20:58 BST

Sam Mendes. And maybe Daniel Craig.

From Dad **to** Harry
12 July 21:02 BST

Trust me – this guy is better for Jessica's career.

CHAPTER TWENTY-SIX
THE FINAL CURTAIN

From Harry **to** Charley
19 July 09:02 GMT BST

OMG – You will not BELIEVE what happened to me last night. I ACTED.

From Charley t**o** Harry
19 July 01:04 PDT

In what?

From Harry **to** Charley
19 July 09:05 GMT BST

The school play.

From Charley **to** Harry
19 July 01:07 PDT

You make an idiot of yourself?

_____

From Harry **to** Charley
19 July 09:07 BST

No.

_____

From Charley **to** Harry
19 July 01:08 PDT

How did you manage that?

_____

From Harry **to** Charley
19 July 09:09 BST

Luck, maybe.

_____

From Charley **to** Harry
19 July 01:11 PDT

That's GREAT – what happened?

_____

From Harry **to** Charley.
19 July 09:22 BST

OK. So like thirty minutes before the school play
starts, Ed Bigstock tells Mr Forbes he wants
ME to take his role cos he's sprained his ankle
falling down some stairs and he can't even

stand without crutches.

So I say, "Don't be crazy, I can't do that, I'm not an actor" – but the next thing I know Mr Forbes and Jessica are giving me this pep talk about how this is my big chance to be a star. "No thanks," I say. But then Jessica says, "Please, Harry, can you do this for me? I know you don't want to do it, but if you don't, we'll have to cancel."

Well, I really, REALLY didn't want to do it, so I gave it one last shot. I said, "Look, Jessica. I'm not the Pumpernickel. I'm just Harry. I play video games. That's my thing. That's what I'm GREAT at doing," but Jessica looks at me and she says, "But you can do this, Harry. So what if you game all the time and everyone thinks you're a little geek? Now's the chance to show everybody what I know you can do."

As you can imagine, she's not exactly ringing my bells with that kind of talk, but I start to think – *Does everybody think I'm just a gamer?* I know that's what my mum thinks. And my sister. And probably Spencer. In fact, every kid in my class probably thinks that's ALL I like doing and is all I EVER do, but that got me feeling that maybe I should try and show 'em I'm not JUST the gamer kid who can get like SEVEN ELITE GAMING PRESTIGES WITH QUICK SCOPE (I got my seventh two days ago – which, BTW, is the max). That's maybe ONE thing I can do – but I can do other stuff too. And maybe now was the time to do it. For Jessica. For my mum. Maybe even for me. So when she said, "I'll be there to help you, Harry. Please?" I said, "You know what? OK. I'll give it a try, why not?"

So Jessica gets all the cast together and she says,

"Brilliant news, everybody! Harry has agreed to play the Pumpernickel!" Not one kid cheered. To be honest, I don't think anybody thought it was a good call having me instead of Ed, but Ed was backstage on crutches and I was there, and the hall was filling up with parents, so there wasn't a lot of choice unless Mr Forbes wanted to do it, which he didn't. I get one "Good luck, Harry, you'll be great" from Oscar da Silva (who was playing evil Citizen Chauvelin and is like the only person who thought I might not crash and burn besides Jessica), and then Jessica's mum gives me my wardrobe (she was wardrobe lady) and it's like HUMONGOUS cos Ed is a GIANT compared to me (and eleven months older). So I'm looking at his costume and I'm thinking, *This is going to be really bad and I'm going to look like an idiot, but you know what? It's for Jessica.*

So then Mr Forbes says, "Five minutes!" And that's when I hear my dad laughing on the other side of the curtain with his friend Tom Witherspoon and I suddenly think, *OMG – what have I just agreed to do? What if I choke and make a complete idiot of myself? What if this is the most embarrassing thing I'm ever going to do in my WHOLE life?* So I get changed and my stomach was like a knot and it started to hurt and that's when I realised I better get to the bathroom because I was feeling so nervous.

So I run to the bathroom at the back and I trip over cos Ed's trousers are too long, but I get to the bathroom and when I flush I hear this terrible bubbling and banging sound coming from the pipes. Then I see the bowl start to fill up with WATER. And now I'm thinking, *Oh my god, it's gonna flood – what do I do?* But it stops

JUST before it reaches the lip. *That was close*, I think. But now I hear Mr Forbes yelling for me because the play is about to begin. So I run back to the stage, but I don't get a chance to tell Mr Forbes about the bathroom cos the curtain is going up and everybody is calling for me to get on stage. So I rush out front as Spencer starts playing the piano and as soon as I get out there I FREEEEEEEEZE. Like I've been nailed to the spot. I can't move. And I don't know what to do cos I can barely breathe. So I just stand there like an idiot.

Well, the hall is packed with PARENTS – all looking at me, waiting for me to say something. I see my mum sitting in the front row with my dad, my sister and my dad's friend Tom and I can see they're all thinking, *What the hell is Harry doing up on that stage?* But I can't wave or smile or even move, cos I'm completely frozen. Then Jessica comes out and she says, "Sir Percy?" And I look at her and I have no idea what I'm meant to say. My mind is a total blank.

"Sir Percy!" she says again to me. Still nothing. And now I'm starting to shake. I can feel my leg going. So Jessica shouts: "SIR PERCY!!!" And that's when I look over and see Mr Forbes pulling his hair out, and I'm thinking, *I really, really have to get out of here. This has been a terrible, terrible, terrible mistake.* And I'm just about to run off stage when I see Ed Bigstock appear behind Mr Forbes and he's pointing at me and laughing and saying, "YOU LOSER!" And that's when I knew he did this to me on purpose, cos he didn't have his crutches.

Well, you know what? I never thought I'd say

this, but thank god for Ed Bigstock. If that kid hadn't been there to make fun of me and try and get even for showing him up in Latin, I would have bailed right there and then. But seeing him standing behind Mr Forbes laughing at me made me forget how nervous I was, cos I got so

mad with him my brain cleared and suddenly I could remember EVERYTHING I had to say and EVERYTHING I had to do. So I turn to Jessica and I say, "Madame St Just? Sir Percy Blakeney!! At your most humble service, ma'am!" And this takes Jessica completely by surprise, cos I think she thought I was going to bunk, so she smiles and then I did the bow thing they did back in those days. But because Ed's sleeves were so long, when I bowed they dragged on the floor and I tripped over 'em standing up, so the next thing I know, I've fallen over again and I'm lying on the stage at Jessica's feet and she's looking down at me in horror and I'm thinking, *I knew this was too good to last.* But then this amazing thing happened.

THE AUDIENCE STARTED LAUGHING!!!!

Like it was the most funny thing they had
ever seen, cos they thought I'd fallen over ON
PURPOSE. Because that's the kind of thing Sir
Percy does in his clever disguise as a prize idiot.
So now me and Jessica see we have everybody in
the hall laughing WITH us not AT US and Jessica
suddenly smiles down at me and nods and I smile

back and I look over and I see Ed cursing and I think, *This may end up being all right after all.*

So we do the first act and it finishes and we come off stage and Ed's standing there and I can tell he's like pretty angry that I'm doing OK, so he says to Mr Forbes, "Why don't I take it from here? My ankle feels good now. There's the sword fight, the chase through the audience, the swinging from the chandeliers – lots of action stuff, which Harry can't do because he's a geek." But Mr Forbes says he doesn't want to make the change. He wants me to finish the play, because I'm doing good and the audience like me – if I WANT to finish. *You must be joking,* I think. *Why push your luck?* That's what I was thinking. But before I can answer, Jessica says, "Don't go. You're MUCH better than Ed!"

So I go back out on stage and now I'm thinking, *How am I going to do all that action stuff? It's going to be a disaster*. But just as I get up on the balcony to do my first leap, Ed Bigstock comes to my rescue and floods the bathroom! The whole hall had to be emergency evacuated before we all got cholera. It was great! The hall STANK! And when we make it outside and my mum and my dad are getting the car, Jessica gives me this HUGE hug and tells me that no matter what, I'll always be her leading man. Then her mum said they had to go so we said goodbye, but I was like, *Wow. Did that really just happen to me?* That was like the best night of my life.

But I don't know if I'll ever see Jessica again, cos next term I think I'm definitely moving schools.

Harry

From Charley **to** Harry

20 July 01:25 PDT

That sucks but guess what? *Eat The Parents* has 76 views. It's going viral!!! Way to go, you little geek!

CHAPTER TWENTY-SEVEN

GOING VIRAL

HIS ROYAL HARRINESS

Tresinkum Farm
Cornwall PL36 0BH
23rd July

Her Majesty the Queen
Buckingham Palace
London SW1 1AA

Your Majesty, hi there (again)

Sorry for not keeping in touch, but life has been
full of all kinds of twists and turns and, to be
honest with you, I didn't know how it was all
going to end up, but I do now so I thought I'd
bring you up to speed with our news, in case
you were worried.

You know I told you how I thought we might have to lose our house cos my dad was having a bad time at work? Well, guess what? You know that movie he wrote that went straight to DVD and then became a download? Well, he had this deal where Alison Hardman wouldn't pay him for all his work, so they let him have the download money and it's now been downloaded like a ton of times by kids with laptops, so my dad has got money again. (Which is just what my mum said would happen. Kind of.)

Plus, the movie me and Walnut made? *Eat the Parents*? Well that DID go viral and now me, my dad and Walnut have got a meeting with Alison Hardman to talk about making our show for TV which means maybe we'll have to go out to America. Yay! So now it looks like they're going back into business together to make MY animated TV show about zombies, which you've got to check out when it's done (and I'll give you a heads-up when we know what time it's going to be on TV).

All of which means my dad can STOP working at the SuperSave, and we're NOT going to lose our house, and I'm gonna stay in my school, which is really great cos I don't want to go to Mount Doom and never see Jessica again. So all in all, things have definitely got a LOT better for this family, since the last time I wrote.

But if you are ever down here in Cornwall and you want to drop by for a cup of tea or something? I know my mum would be happy to see you because my mum still finds it pretty boring living in the country (she's from the city) and she's always saying how much she enjoys meeting fun and interesting new people. You don't have to call, just turn up – you'll always be welcome in our house (although it might be better if you DID call, in case she hasn't done the dishes). And if you wanted to bring your dogs, I could easily walk them for you (as long as they don't go down rabbit holes).

Anyway, I do hope you visit and we can meet one day, cos you're like the first person I ever wrote to who was kind enough to write back to me apart from my cousin (who only wrote back cos his dad made him) and also the Prime Minister. So thanks a lot for that, Your Majesty, and when you see the Prime Minister, please say thanks to him too.

Good luck and have fun.

Harry Riddles

ACKNOWLEDGEMENTS

Lots of people have given me a lot of help, love and support over the years. My good friends Johnny Bamford, Steff Hocken and Jack Goldsby-West, who help fight the fires on an almost daily basis. Our families. Kate and Anna at Abner Stein's office. Harriet and all at HarperCollins for great editorial advice and support. And my lovely Gemma.

Thank you all.